I0576028

The Lies I Tell My Friends

TALLY JOHNSON

e-book ISBN-13: 979-8-9930812-7-4

Paperback ISBN-13: 979-8-9930812-6-7

Cover design by: Susan Roddey

Edited by: Lynn Picknett

Layout by: Jason Roach

Printed in the United States of America

Dedication

This book is dedicated to my beloved wife, Rachel, without whom none of this would have ever happened, and the rest of my family; I love all y'all.

It is also dedicated to my late brother Brennan Johnson and my late Father-in-law Alex Wylie, both of whom always encouraged me to keep going in all things regardless.

Special shout-outs to Christopher Lawson aka Captain Smiley, the founding father of Palmetto State Hangers who shows all of us how we should aspire to be, and to Carol Cowles, the first con programming person who let me tell my lies at ConCarolinas and then let me come back and do them again.

"DON'T KNOW ..."

Don't know much but folklore and history,

Especially JFK and ghosties

(And other people not alive today).

I know a little about the biology and

Enough about the chemistry

To know when sparks fly,

Flames will follow.

I know what the poets say

And tho I can't say it

As well as they;

I'll say it still -

I love YOU and I always will.

Introduction

What's All the Hub, Bub?

This book, like all my others, is my wife Rachel's fault and I mean that in the very best possible sense, I promise. As of this writing, we've been married for twenty-four years and she is very much my muse, and a much better writer than I am or likely will be. But the whole story-telling thing and the books that have sprung from it are her fault regardless. Back when she was still toiling in the vineyard that is public education in South Carolina, she decided early on to be the teacher who put on the best Halloween parties EVER. However, she needed a way to distract the kids so she could get the food ready. Since I was a good husband and could take time off, I was drafted to be the distraction. Now, I

1

thought just being there in the flesh would suffice, but nope, I was to entertain some twenty-odd kids getting ramped up for a sugar high... BEFORE she invited her unit mates and their three other classes of twenty each. GULP. I can't sing and I sure enough can't dance... but I can talk, and I talk funny, even for a Southerner. And I know a thing or two about ghosts... ghosts are Halloween stuff... I'll tell a few piddling stories, eat my pizza and drink some punch and then take off. Yeah, not even close. I talked for a solid forty-five minutes, and the kids would have almost rather have listened to me than eat pizza. The wife and her coworkers were over the moon for the rest and that was that...I was the designated storyteller every Halloween henceforth. I must have been tolerable: kids would come back even after leaving second or third grade to hear the same ole same ole.

My poor wife also has to bear the blame for the books. After my debut as a storyteller (junior grade), I began to cuss about all the very, very many ghost story books I kept buying had the same two or three stories from South Carolina. Rachel bore this well for a few months and finally told me to write one. I knew loads and loads of stories and folks seemed to like them and she knew folks would buy the book. Naturally, I scoffed. No one with any sense would publish a book written by a guy from the mill hill of Lyman, much less buy one. Well, four books of ghost lore from South Carolina, a short story anthology, and another half dozen short stories later, she was right and I was wrong, like most husbands wind up being.

Anyhoo, the whole storytelling thing stayed mainly a Halloween distraction for a few years, then Rachel and I and some friends went to Dragon Con so I could meet one of my idols, Harlan Ellison. I was gobsmacked to find my tribe... nerds, geeks, Goths, and all the rest. I noticed that there were even panels on the paranormal. So, when those same friends mentioned that Charlotte had a fandom con, I decided to apply on a lark... and I got accepted as an author guest. I had a blast, sold some books, and got asked back. After a year or two, I mentioned I could do ghost stories and asked if I could move to the paranormal track, since my only two books were ghost non-fiction. They said yes to both, and I packed a panel room at nine p.m. on Friday. That first trip to ConCarolinas led to me doing cons in four states for the last dozen years and to being lucky enough to share a stage with some dear friends and amazing musicians more than once. Of course, the more gigs I did, the better I got at telling my tales, so everyone said, at least.

Since this is my introduction, I'll ramble a bit if I want and the context will help y'all understand why me being a professional storyteller is such an honest achievement.

According to my parents, I didn't talk until I was three. I was reading at two, but speech… meh. And I had two strikes against me out of the gate…one, I had a thick Southern accent. Even thicker than sweet tea and fried chicken. Second, I had a metric butt-ton of speech defects. Sounds like S, CH, TH, SH, C, K and likely some I've forgotten about all came out the same. Add in the fact that most of my vocabulary came from print and I was damned near incomprehensible to anyone who wasn't family. I did speech therapy until eighth grade, then I escaped. When I get tired and/or have a few drinks, the accent gets super thick and if I let my brain outpace my tongue or vice versa, the defects still creep in too. To top all that off, I'm basically very, very shy around strangers. So, all you folks who've sat through midnight con panels and midnight bacon listening to me, I really appreciate it more than you'll ever know.

At any rate, while I'm getting paid gigs at schools and libraries all over the Carolinas, me and my best friend Bill decided we needed to get in shape, so we'd start camping and hiking. He convinced me to try hammocks, since I had a bad back and barking knees. That was a most excellent idea. We've managed to get out to the woods five or six times a year, health and real life permitting. He tended to hang out on hammocksforums.com and look for campsites and trails and the like. He found a bunch of folks from South Carolina who were getting together at Sesquicentennial State Park in Columbia, so we decided to check it out. That was the formal birth of a group of nuts called Palmetto State Hangers, one of the biggest and best hammock camping groups in the US. At some point around the campfire, either he, or more likely I, mentioned that I wrote books of true ghost stories and I even told them for money sometimes. Some kind soul asked me to tell one and an hour later, I finally hushed. Every PSH event since until the past year, I told tales twice a weekend and some folks came from as far away as Kentucky and Louisiana to hear them… Still blows my feeble mind.

At any rate, I'm going to shush and "tell" y'all some of my favorites. All of these stories have a basis in fact, well, folklore anyway. The versions that follow are best experienced either with Braxton Ballew of Valentine Wolfe improvising on his double bass in a dark hotel conference room or around a blazing pallet fire while tree frogs sing and hammocks sway in the breeze.

Part One:

Whoppers with a Hint

of Wood Smoke

A Face in the Hammock

This story is a fairly recent addition to my repertoire of fireside lies.

About three years ago, me and Rooster (my buddy Bill, it's a long story) decided we'd do the Peak to Prosperity Passage of the Palmetto Trail and make use of the campsite about halfway so he could test out some new gear. Now, Rooster does love him some hammock gear. The boy must have enough to equip a whole platoon. But it was an old rail line turned hiking trail. So, it was flat with a bunch of creek crossings, so I figured it would be a pleasant change from our usual death treks straight uphill both ways. Yeah right. Normally, I sleep pretty danged well in my hammock. That becomes important later.

It was a classic late spring day in South Carolina. Eighty

in the shade, no breeze and as humid as Satan's... armpit. So by the time we reached the campsite, I was thoroughly whupped. I had sweated through my clothes and somebody else's. The map said ten miles round trip, but I said it was nearer to fifty and my knees and back thought I was right. Rooster just kept walking along, earbuds firmly in to drown out my unique combination of bitching and gasping. We set up our hammocks and tarps about an hour before dark and ate supper sitting on the picnic table. We both mentioned that it was supposed to start raining sideways about eight in the morning so we needed to get up and be as close to the car as we could get before then. Usually, one or the other of us is up at the butt crack of dawn and rouses the other one. I figured if we got up at six-ish, we'd be less than a mile from the car if not in the car by the time the weather turned. Yeah, not so bloody much. Anyway, we shot the bull and looked around for a few minutes, then we decided to get in our hammocks, zip up our bug nets and listen to our iPods until either the batteries crapped out or we passed out before the skeeters ate us down to the bone. The surroundings weren't as scenic as our usual spots up at Burrell's Ford and some others, but still better than being trapped inside. The creek was mostly stagnant, hence the skeeter orgy and we had cow pastures on three sides just past the little fringe of a tree line. The side nearest my hammock was a newly plowed but thankfully not mucked field… that'll be important here in a second.

Now, even after drinking all the caffeine in the tri-state, I usually sleep like the faithful dead in my hammock. Now, the allergy pills help, but normally I'm good for at least seven hard hours. However, this was certainly one of the exceptions. Part of it was the utter absence of anything even close to a breeze. Part of it was the bug net. Even attached, it sags just enough to scrape my chin when I toss and turn before I finally go under. At any rate, the iPod died about ten and my bladder got full about then too. So I hopped up and made my way to the nearest free tree. The night was gorgeous, if a bit too muggy for my taste. A couple of high puffy clouds streaking by a full moon hanging just over the tops of the dogwoods along the creek. Rooster was gently snoring along as Wille sang about Blue Eyes Cryin'. I need to teach the boy to put some bass on that… A handful of tree frogs were finishing one last chorus, and a barn owl screeched somewhere down the trail, drowning out the whisper of semis on the interstate. A typical night in the trees so far. I hopped back under my quilt and drifted off with a minimum of wiggling.

For some ungodly reason, my eyes popped open right at four. Lord, how I wish they hadn't. I woke up to a face about an inch from mine. Stark white crew cut. Blue rheumy eyes staring unblinking behind thick bifocals. A whisp of a mustache and about three days' growth. Of course, the ragged gash running the length of his corrugated forehead all the way to the bone threw me off a bit, as did the fact that he looked to be upside down to my sleep-smeared eye. After a beat trying to process the damned near impossible, it dawned on me that his ugly mug was dripping blood onto my chin and that he'd had to tear my tarp and my bug net. Which, trust me, to somebody as poor and cheap as I am, is grounds for a throwdown at any hoedown. So, I sat up and began to choose which cuss words I was going to deploy first. About then I realized that nothing was torn, I was still in my hammock, and that I was as alone as I was at the start. But where the hell had the man come from and where the happy hell did he go? So I hopped up - well as close as my stove-up ass can get to it, dug my cigarettes out of the ridgeline organizer, and decided that I was up for the duration. I dug the beer I had forgotten to drink out of my pack and gingerly did a lap of the camp looking for any sign of mister man. Not even a drop of blood on my tarp. Nary a footprint in the dust. Just some fresh deer scat over near the bear pole. I knew trying to rouse Rooster would be as productive as trying to hatch a plastic Easter egg, so I plopped my big behind on the picnic table and chain smoked until first light.

After a positively gross, as in we got sweaty enough to give Frosty a terminal case of swamp ass "stroll" back to the car in a hellacious thunder boomer, we headed to eat at the nearest awful Waffle. I mentioned that I slept for shit, but Rooster just grunted, so I decided not to bore him with my exploits. I don't recommend sitting in a Waffle House off the interstate soaked to the bone in dirty hiking clothes. Some of the looks I got would have curdled powdered coffee creamer. Not to mention that I damned near froze. I mean, who runs the blasted AC on sixty-five degrees in a thunderstorm?

Monday at work, I decided to do some digging into my new friend. Turns out back in the Fifties, the man that owned the plowed tract behind us had died when his tractor threw an axle, tossing him ass over teakettle under the rear tire. He staggered to the railroad right of way and tried to flag down the train but died before it came. I can only guess he'd never seen a fool in a hammock before or was wondering what was making all that racket, so he took a quick peek. One of these days, we'll need to go back.

Booger Jim

For some reason, a young fan (yes, I have a few, now shush) loves this particular story. It's more an urban legend than a true ghost story, but who am I to deny a fan, especially one who's read and bought all my stuff to the point she can do requests?

Up near Blacksburg over by Gaffney, the Highway Twenty-Nine bridge over Broad River used to have character. It was an old steel bridge with the girders up top and dated back to the 1930s at least. Now they've torn it down for a functional and ugly concrete span. Pfui on that noise. Now, the old bridge was the hangout of a local boogeyman known as Booger Jim. Booger Jim was a tragic figure, I expect. One reason I feel safe in saying that is the rumor that he was the offspring of some poor lass known only as the county whore and a bull. Yes, you read that right - and no, I didn't make it up. He was known to drink a bit...

15

a jar at a time, and lived on the Blacksburg side of the river in a shack with his wife, who did not approve of his carrying on in his cups. So they were prone to having some slobber-knocker throwdowns, most of which Jim lost and slept off on the riverbank under the old bridge. Well, according to legend, one night Jim and his missus had a bit more violent fight than usual and Jim came out the worse for it, but he did smack her around a bit more than usual. This night, she followed him to the bridge and let him fall into the sleep only known to professional drinkers and those about to have major surgery. When he was good and gone, she tied a set of jumper cables around his neck and dragged him up to the road. Now, I assume Jim was either on the jagged edge of alcohol poisoning or was already dead, because I can't imagine a body being hauled along by the neck not waking up ready to raise all manner of hell. Of course, why folks who from all accounts didn't have a car would have a set of jumper cables plumb evades me. At any rate, she tied the other end of the cables to the bridge's guardrail and shoved Jim over the side. And end scene, one would think...

And, since I'm telling it, you'd be wrong. Jim was prone to show up on the old bridge on rainy nights when the moon was new. He'd stomp up the centerline coming from the Gaffney side, heedless of any traffic, until he reached the end of the span where he'd vanish as soon as he stepped over.

Of course, before I-85 was built, I expect the long-haul truckers running from Atlanta to Charlotte were rather unhappy at dealing with this. The narrow bridge on a wet two- lane road in the pitch black known only as country dark was bad enough, but to add in some drunk stomping up the road like it was his driveway was likely about more than they could bear.

Since I pride myself on actually going to the sites I write about in my non-fiction, a visit to Booger Jim was required. Thankfully, the old bridge was still there when I went with my wife and another couple. The road is still narrow and still as dark as week-old coffee as soon as the sun sets. We found a wide spot on the shoulder just up the road from the bridge and me and my buddy Michael trotted down there, praying that all the traffic would stay on I-85 for a bit. Now, to conjure up Booger Jim, you're supposed to holler his name three times from the center of the bridge. According to the legend, he'll rustle the nearby underbrush and then appear on the Gaffney side, preceded by the stink of one-eighty proof shine. Well, we did what we were supposed to do but all we conjured up was an overweight semi dodging the weigh station at the state line. Now, I ain't sure if Booger Jim still bothers to visit the new bridge. Y'all will have to ride over yonder and let me know.

Crybaby Bridge

Ah yes, Crybaby Bridge. Every amateur ghost hunter's first stop and the bane of mothers of teens everywhere. There really isn't a set version but the basics are fairly intact. During a war, usually World War II or Vietnam, though I have heard the Civil War mentioned a time or two, a sweet innocent young bride strays due to either loneliness or boredom, and on occasion for financial gain. It always happens about a year before the brave soldier husband is due to return from active combat duty on the other side of the world. The poor wife gets pregnant and has the baby. The couple always have a farm off the beaten path and on the other side of a creek or river prone to erratic flooding. Finally, happy days are here again! The husband is coming home in a week according to his last letter and his buddy has convinced him to buy a new motorcycle with his separation bonus. He'll be in on the late train on the nearest Friday or Saturday.

Of course the wife is overjoyed… until she looks in the cradle at her three-month-old child. Hubby will NOT be pleased about this at all. Then she starts to justify herself. HE probably went to a whorehouse over there. He'll understand that a young woman has needs too. The raise was worth it at the plant. She had to pay the bills after all. Besides, he's always wanted a son, and she'll make the math work. He wasn't a whiz at school and he'll be thrilled to see her regardless. It'll be just fine.

Finally, the fateful night! But he's held up. The train is delayed by the nasty weather, and all the troops have made the train make extra stops. She gets worried and walks down to the old bridge. She's always wanted to ride on a fancy motorcycle. It'll give her a chance to explain about the baby too. He loves kids. Off they go into the worse storm in a century. Hauntings like this don't happen due to good weather, ya know.

Finally, here comes the headlight and she can hear the horn blaring. How sweet… he's telling her he's coming home and almost there. But the road is slicker than goose shit on glass. And what the hell is that white shape in the road? Being a new rider, he panics and lays the bike down and slides into the figure in white. Oh LORD! It's a girl with a babe in arms. Mama goes over one side and the baby goes over the other. Splash, splash, gurgle, gurgle. Our hero goes down to the creek bank to check on the lady who fell and finds her drowned and or with her skull bashed in by a convenient rock. He realizes that the body is his bride, and he goes to their love nest and kills himself.

Pretty standard issue ghost story, right? Now it gets to be interesting. Flash forward a decade or so. A young man's thoughts turn to love - or at the very least, lust. He and his girlfriend are long past ready to get physical but living at home with nosy parents seems to be a perpetual cock block. During a chat in the locker room, the talk turns to everyone's latest conquest. Our bundle of overflowing hormones gets the usual business about being a virgin and etc. But he has heard tell of this creepy bridge out in the back of beyond where a bunch of guys have taken their girlfriends to get lucky. And the wheels turn. This Friday, he'll wine and dine his love and then get lucky finally.

It's easy really. You drive down this long dark stretch of one lane blacktop to this rickety old bridge. No houses within a dozen miles. The poor girl will be scared out of her wits by the dark and the story about the poor cheating wife and her brave soldier. Then you park on the bridge, right in the middle. Ain't ever any traffic or nosy neighbors. You roll down the windows and either honk the horn three times or flash the lights. Then the young mother either appears on the bridge or screams for her baby from the creek below. Then the girl you're with jumps into your lap and you're in like Flynn.

Now, I hate to disappoint you budding ghost hunters, but all of the above is a lie. Ain't no woman with an illegitimate baby. Ain't no dashing war hero husband. You have city kids in country dark, no ambient glow from the streetlights. No light pollution from a dozen mini-malls on the bypass. No traffic noise, just tree frogs, crickets, maybe a deer snorting in disgust at being awakened again. The mother, being made up, never shows. That flash of white could be that retreating deer or a bird diving for bugs. Or just imagination. Crybaby Bridge exists solely to get teenagers laid. Yes, YOURS is the real one and your mom's best friend from high school sister's ex-boyfriend swore he knew the couple in question. BULLSHIT. It's just a story.

Devil's Tramping Ground

I really need to quit telling this one. The hook is that my crazy assed mouth has apparently written a check that my fat arse will have to cash real soon. See, there's a little garden spot up near Siler City, North Carolina called the Devil's Tramping Ground, a kissin' cousin to the Devil's Stomping Ground over near Forty Acre Rock in Lancaster County, South Carolina. But regardless, my demented self made the claim in public that I had plans for my 50th birthday… which was in 2022 for those of y'all who want to do your shopping now. Late presents will still be accepted. But first, let me explain what the deal is and y'all decide for yourselves if I really need to freeze my ass off on the cold, cold ground. Sadly, real life and the hangover from that whole pesky pandemic thing conspired to not let the planned hootenanny occur. Maybe for my 60th…

The Devil's Tramping Ground is reputedly one of the

spots where Ole Nick himself, Satan, comes to Earth to pace all night and decide what new mischief to unleash on humanity. Hopefully, his well is running dry after the last few years. The soil in a circular area about an acre around is sterile about ten feet wide in a loop on the outside edge, but there's a small stand of trees in the center. Items left on the path, ranging in size from a beer can to a railroad crosstie, are found moved violently out of the way at first light.

So, my big mouth at cons all over the Southeast and at hammock hangs all over South Carolina has announced that for the big Five Oh I would be staked down in a mummy sleeping bag(don't go scouring YouTube for the video - real life conspired against this happening as planned)... leaving only my ugly mug visible to the wider world. And, because go big or go home, the bag would be staked with ten penny nails around the edges, just in case I decided to try to inchworm my way out of it... like my ragged back and knees and oversized gut would allow that anyway. The best part is my best friend Rooster would film it and likely livestream it all over social media. Yup, you could see my tonnage get punted by Satan himself.... Or watch him break a hoof or two. Y'all could have some sympathy for me at least. I mean, I expect he gets plenty thanks to Mick Jagger and them...

Kings Mountain

and the King's Messengers

Now, I promised myself that I wouldn't go down the research rabbit hole for this book. So, y'all can get *Ghosts of the South Carolina Upcountry* or any good book on the American Revolution to get the history of the actual battle. I mean, c'mon y'all, just let me lie awhile, like it says on the tin, as it were.

At any rate, the battle of Kings Mountain happened in October 1780. It should serve as a lesson in why you don't threaten rednecks. Or hillbillies. Or their descendants. General Cornwallis, having just received the surrender of Charleston, figured that the submission of the rest of the southeast would follow in due course. Of course, the backcountry settlers in the Carolinas and Tennessee had no great love for Charleston or the British Army either. They had their hands full with angry Cherokee and their allies. Then Cornwallis went stupid. He sent a proclamation to the backcountry settlers in the Carolinas and the Overmountain men in Tennessee demanding they swear allegiance to the Crown or "Join my forces or I will come to you: hang your leaders, burn your homes and lay waste to your land." by way of Major Patrick Ferguson. Well, he got their undivided attention, and they said, more or less, "Like Hell you will." So they decided to meet up with Ferguson and settle their disagreement like gentlemen. Yeah right... they decided that Ferguson needed an ass-whipping and that they'd oblige. Well, Ferguson, he got to Kings Mountain right near the border of North and South Carolina and, like Obi-Wan, got the high ground on the crest of the hill. Sadly, the high ground does better for light sabers than it does for muskets. The Overmountain men came up the hill from tree to tree and wiped out a large swath of Ferguson's Tories. Yup, the only British soldier at Kings Mountain was the Major himself. Everyone else was an American.

Now, Ferguson had brass balls the size of a house. He was the only officer mounted and wore a blue and white plaid vest... basically saying here I am! And the Overmountain boys took careful note...they shot him slap full of lead. If memory serves, he was hit at least seven times and cut down at least that many white flags waved by his beaten troops. The rebels won the battle, captured or killed most of Ferguson's command, and then headed home. They did respect the Major enough to build a cairn over his body... and christened it in the old Scottish way. Hint, that ain't with lemonade. Now, as to why Ferguson's request to Cornwallis in Charlotte for reinforcements went unheeded, that's a tale for in a minute.

Now, if you go to Kings Mountain National Military Park, the rangers and park attendants will tell you double-quick, ain't never ever been any ghosts hereabouts... because the National Park Service says so. But, if you're lucky enough to walk the trail just about dark in early October or take part in the reenactment of the battle, you may have a bit different tale to tell. Folks have heard gunshots and smelled gunpowder in the trees. Folks have seen figures running from tree to tree but never emerging from the next. There have been reports of reenactors having lanterns blown out on the trail and being pushed by invisible hands.

My favorite tale happened to my niece when we visited the park. It was a steamy August Saturday afternoon and she decided to come with me and my in-laws as I got my history nerd on and got some exercise to boot. We did the trail, and

I added my two cents to every sign and marker. At the bottom of the hill, me and Katie were a bit ahead of the rest and I told her about why Ferguson rated a cairn and everyone else was food for wolves and scavengers and how they christened it. Hey, you try explaining peeing on a fallen foe to a kid in grammar school. I was on one side and she was across from me, humoring me as much as she could, when she told me to stop! I said what? And she accused me of hitting her in the ear with an acorn. Y'all have seen me talk when I'm interested, I'm all **hands. Trust** me, I didn't do a thing for once. But I half turned and saw a guy in a blue and white plaid vest and fiery red hair giving us both a **pure go-to-hell** smirk. As I turned all the way around and said KATIE! He stepped INTO an oak tree. Not around, not behind, but INTO. I knew then that Major Ferguson still didn't like Americans. Of course, the in-laws came up and that was the end of all that.

Now, about those reinforcements that Ferguson didn't get. Well, he sent two messengers to **Charlotte Town, as it was known then,** to update Cornwallis and request any men he could spare. Of course, he sent two fellows that in hindsight weren't the best for the job. You see, legend has it that en route to Kings Mountain, Ferguson stopped at a tavern on the Catawba River and two of his men had a disagreement with the keeper. The keeper came out the

worst in the dispute and wound up in the river with a sizable hole in his skull, leaving a rather upset widow and several small children. Now fast forward about a week if you're the widow. You've just buried your husband and you're running a tavern in the back of beyond and the two sumbitches who murdered your husband ride up and demand beer and food. Of course, you draw two beers and spoon out some stew... and bash both their brains out all over the table. Then you drag their bodies to the river. Payback is a **bitch.**

Fast forward about two hundred years... and this part may or may not be a bit... exaggerated. My uncle, the coolest guy I knew as an eight-year-old, went to USC Columbia, rode a motorcycle and drove a '65 Mustang, and took me to concerts... like P-Funk in the old Charlotte Coliseum. After the concert was over, which blew my feeble little redneck mind. I mean, a six-foot six black guy playing the bass coming out of an egg in a wedding gown...damn. But it did smell funny. Like a skunk's ass and burnt coffee. At any rate, we stopped just past the airport to eat at Waffle House and my uncle asked how traffic was heading to Spartanburg. The waitress told him that I-85 South was closed down about the state line because of a bad wreck, so we should just sit tight. Ah, by my uncle said he knew a short cut. Now, with a few more miles behind me, if someone says that to you and you ain't driving... get out of the damned car. Ain't nothing good ever came from a short cut... unless I'm driving, natch. Then, it meant more time on the back of the Honda, so I was down as dirt with the idea. We jumped off the interstate and headed out towards Boiling Springs or somewhere with more trees than people. After about a half hour, we hit a T-intersection. The road faced a white rail fence with the big yellow sign with the black arrow on it under a flickering streetlight. Two guys were standing under the light looking at a map **and** holding horses by the reins. I've seen weirder shit after midnight, but not then. My uncle, being a good Southern boy, hollered if they needed a hand. Then they looked up and I tried to climb into my uncle's helmet. The shorter guy had one eye missing and a worm peeked out from the black socket. His scalp was peeled back and showed a lovely swath of skull. And most of his lower jaw was gone. The taller one had no nose and what looked to be a nest of roaches for a beard. The greenish pallor of his face made him look as bad as his buddy. One of them asked my uncle, "Which way to Charlotte Town?" My uncle, who apparently didn't notice how pretty they were, simply gestured over his shoulder and said, "Head for the lights. Can't miss it." They mounted, nodded, and headed off hard to the right. My uncle shook his head, muttered something about damned drunks and off we went to the left. I think I crawled out of his helmet about the time we passed the Peachoid aka the big sunburnt butt in Gaffney.

Larry Stevens

I've been a confirmed hammock hanger for about eight years now. Given the shape my knees and back are in, I'll never go back to being a ground-dweller. If I did, y'all would have to find a crane to hoist my stove-up ass back upright after one night. But, back in my younger days, I did camp and hike some. After high school graduation, I decided to take a week and head for the high country. I figured I'd do a night or two up at Burrell's Ford and wade out to Ellicott Rock, then head up to Pisgah. Maybe do Graveyard Fields. I'd try to get to Roan Mountain to hear the choir if I got lucky. But first, I had to drive through the usual. Raining sideways. Wind howling, making the truck shimmy like a cheerleader. Thunder and lightning to beat the band and damned near drowning out the radio. Oh well. Now, this trip seems to have set the pattern for every hike I've done since. It pours and storms either the night before or the morning I head out, especially if Rooster is with me and he about always is.

Anyways, I'm bombing up State Highway 107 singing along to AC/DC when I see a middle-aged guy hitching a ride. Blond crew cut, tan trench coat, gray slacks and what used to be penny loafers. Given that I ain't passed or even seen another car since I left Walhalla, I figured I was his only chance to get dry. Being a good southern boy, I stopped and popped the door open. I hollered "Need a ride, man?" He nodded and climbed in. He said he was parked up at the Spring and thanked me for the ride. That was the end of the conversation. I did turn the tape off, since some folks aren't fans of metal, especially turned up to eleven. Besides, I was saving Hell's Bells for the ride to the Fish Hatchery. A minute or two after I passed the Overlook, I asked him to remind me where his car was. He didn't answer, so I glanced over, thinking he'd dozed off. And damned if he wasn't gone. Seat's as empty as it was when I left Lyman. Except for the pile of sopping wet leaves, mud, and pine needles getting soaked up by my cloth seats. Now, the truck had power windows and power locks, so I'd have noticed if he tried to jump out or some such nonsense. I pulled over at Moody Spring to get my bearings and my mind right… and to open the fresh pack of smokes I'd been saving. It looked like the storm was clearing out but it would be a wet hike in. Damned if I didn't glance down the road and see the back of a brown trench coat walking down to the Overlook. I looked around and I was the only car in sight. I was more than a little bit upset but damned if I was gonna run home with my tail between my legs. Now, I just went on up to Pisgah and found a spot pretty close to the road.

Now, according to books by Nancy Roberts, the nearest thing to a true expert on all things ghostly in South Carolina, Larry Stevens is the gent I picked up some thirty odd years back. He was working on his pilot's license out of what was then Donaldson Airport in Greenville shortly after World War II. On his last solo flight, he flew towards the mountains between Wahalla and Cashiers North Carolina. Understandably, he got a bit distracted by the scenery and ran out of gas, crashing at the base of the mountain just below Moody Springs. It took several days for his body to be found... by humans at least. The local wildlife found it first and enjoyed the unexpected snack.

Now, I'm not saying Nancy Roberts might have stretched this a bit but, there was a plane crash in the same general area in March 1943. A B-25 Army Air Corps plane crashed into a mountain top at night twenty-one miles north of Walhalla and just one mile south of the Fish Hatchery off Highway 107. The crash killed five service members on their way from Meridian, Mississippi, to Donaldson Army Air

Base in Greenville. On March 21, 1943, a fifteen-year-old boy, Seab Crane was riding his horse along Moody Trail to visit his friends near the Fish Hatchery when his horse suddenly became "spooked" by an unknown foreign object on the riding trail. The object turned out to be one of the plane's engines. And that's what led to the discovery of the downed B-25. The weird part of the tale is... no one named Larry Stevens was on that flight. Here is the list of those killed in the crash: Flight Officer, Richard S. Brook, 2nd Lt. Earl S. Monrow, 2nd Lt. Philip J. Graziano, Staff Sgt. Harvey M. Capellman, and Sgt. Michael Sekel. This begs the question... Who the hell is Larry Stevens? And if it wasn't him I picked up, who the Hell was it? I've been back to Burrell's a bunch of times since and thank heavens the weather hasn't been quite shitty enough to inspire Larry to come out and need another ride. Yet.

Rivers Bridge

I especially love telling this story at Palmetto Campout down at Sesquicentennial State Park. Because most every state park ranger in South Carolina comes to help out new campers have a great time on their first camping trip and it lets me violate park policy just a little. Ya see, just like the National Park Service, the South Carolina Department of Parks Recreation and Tourism denies that any site under their care is haunted at all. Well, policy can say that until it gets tired, but we all know it ain't true... You mean the government ain't fully truthful... NO WAY! Just wait a bit if you think that's bad.

This story is one of the few I can't blame on me going looking for trouble, kinda. Ya see, when I was working on *Ghosts of the South Carolina Midlands*, I had the brainstorm to go visit all the sites I was going to use in the book in a day. It's been a minute and if I tried it now, I'd be laid up for a month in traction. It was high August in South Carolina. One hundred degrees in the shade. Not a breath of breeze and the humidity was about a thousand percent. At any rate, I had AC in the car, gas prices were reasonable, the iPod was charged and the wife said not no but hell no to this bit of ridin'. I left about seven in the morning and hit sites from St. Matthews all the way over to Aiken and still had a bunch left to get to. I stopped at a barbeque joint and ate until I just about popped, and I decided I needed a break. Highway hypnosis and bad knees meant that I needed to go walk about for a minute. I had no idea where a good spot was to stretch my legs. Then I came across the sign for Rivers Bridge State Historic Site. I had a vague idea that it was related to the Civil War, so I figured I'd take the chance. I parked and had the whole lot to myself. I headed down the well-marked and well-kept path reading all the markers. After maybe a quarter mile in the shade, the trail came out to a black water swamp. I stood there and lit a cigarette and tried to decide if I really wanted to complete the loop or just go back up the hill when something caught my eye.

It was a quick movement out in the swamp, then a patch of blue. Then a man in what looked like a blue wool jacket wading waist deep in black water. His sudden appearance was made even more jarring when I noticed he was carrying a rifle that looked like an antique. I started to shout for him to get out of there before he got snake bit when he threw his arms out and fell on his back in the water. He didn't make a sound, and the water never splashed or even rippled. Of course, I knew I'd seen a damned ghost. And I wasn't even looking for the damned thing! At least there. I mean, the battle happened in early February, not August. About then I realized that every bird in the area had gone stone silent and had been for the last few minutes, I was all alone. In a swamp. With a ghost I had no idea existed until I saw him. Yeah, the rest of the loop could wait until next time. I headed up the hill and ran into a couple on a motorcycle who were visiting all the Civil War sites they could hit off I-95. They asked how the trail was and I muttered real quiet and took off. Then I headed towards the house. I'd hit what I had needed to and I knew I 'd never top what had just happened. At least on that trip.

Alice of the Hermitage

Every married person has an "approved list." You know, the handful of celebrities your partner would allow you to cheat with. Of course, ninety-nine percent of these lists stay filed away for pillow talk silliness. I know I'll never act on mine. I mean, everyone on it is dead. Jackie Kennedy, Liz Taylor in her prime, Marilyn Monroe. Oh, and a young lady from Pawley's Island down near Georgetown South Carolina named Alice Flagg.

Alice Flagg was the heiress to one of the biggest rice plantations on the Carolina coast before the Civil War. Her older brother, Dr. Allard Flagg, was her co-heir and guardian since her parents were struck down by malaria when she was a toddler. Dr. Flagg was of the old school, namely in the absence of the parents, the word of the older brother was law. As an older brother, back in younger days, I would have fully endorsed this concept. Pity my baby sister and late baby brother were a bit too strong willed for it to fly. Of course, Dr. Flagg took it upon himself to ensure his sister was a worthy bride for a member of the antebellum planter elite and he didn't bother to ask Alice what her thoughts on the matter were. So off Alice went to Madame Tavande's School in Charleston. Now, Madame Tavande still walks the halls of the Sword Gate house on Legare Street making sure none of her other pupils pull the stunt that Alice and another of her classmates pulled.

You see, Alice and a friend of hers were on an outing to the market, much like coeds from the College of Charleston do today. No information is available on whether they wore sundresses and denim jackets or not, or if they were looking for Citadel men. But the outcome was similar. The two young ladies of quality met two men. Both fellows were a bit older and worldly-wise. One was a Yankee tutor to one of Charleston's first families and the one that caught the eye of Miss Flagg was an Irish carpenter named Edward O'Reilly. Well, the two girls were smitten, and the couples were together every opportunity they could seize. The Charleston native caused a bit of a scandal when she took her suitor home and introduced him to her father in hopes of getting the okay to marry him. The father objected, not because the man was a Yankee from Boston but because he wasn't of their class. The daughter, being as headstrong as modern sisters, married him secretly. After about a week, he came to the school and demanded to be allowed to take his wife home. Madame Tavande of course was shocked and demanded that the ladies gather in the main hall and that the culprit reveal herself. Well, she did, much to Mme. Tavande's dismay and left with her husband to live happily ever after.

To Alice's credit, she wasn't quite as brazen in her flaunting of the rules of the society she lived in. She and Patrick decided to get married as well and her friend and her husband served as witnesses, but Alice knew that her brother would not approve of a sudden elopement with a commoner, much less a manual laborer and a foreigner. But she told her husband to be patient and that she'd convince her brother to see things her way over the holiday break. With that, she left Charleston wearing the gold band engraved "With Love to My Wife Alice- EOR" on a gold chain around her neck... next to the pesky mosquito bite on her collarbone.

When Alice arrived back at the family home The Hermitage the weekend before Thanksgiving, her brother immediately rushed her into his study. "Good news, sister mine! I have found you a husband! You recall Mister Allston Belin, don't you? Owns Wachesaw across the river. Now, now, don't fret. I know he's twice your age, but his wife just died in childbirth and the poor man needs an heir. Of course, if you can't provide one, Wachesaw may well come to us as your dowry. The wedding is scheduled for New Years Day, so you need to start making plans now for it."

Of course, having two husbands was just as illegal then as it is now, so Alice did the natural thing. She fainted.

She awoke two days later in a fog. She knew she was in her bed but she didn't feel like herself. After lunch, her brother came in, looking mournful. Yellow fever! But how? She'd left Pawley's before the miasma brought the bad air that bore the fever. She'd never felt better at school... of course, being a secret newlywed had helped. Her brother tried to put a good face on things, but she knew as well as he did what those words meant. Death. She had to get word to Edward and figure out how to explain things to her brother. He loved Alice and she knew he'd love Edward if she could just convince him that things were fine and that love conquered all.

Dr. Flagg was now doubly distraught. His grand plans for doubling his holdings and marrying his sister to the wealthiest planter from Georgetown to Wilmington had just about come to naught. Damned yellow fever! The season had passed. Quinine would hold off the worst of it for a month at most. But at the end, the hallucinations and rambling would start and then death would have to follow. In his desperation, Dr. Flagg didn't just write to all his colleagues; he went to the slave cabins and talked to the root workers and grannies in hopes of finding a way to stop the slow grinding of the wheel of time. But, despite all his efforts, Alice steadily got worse and by Christmas, the end stage had arrived. In faint hopes of controlling the spiking fever, Dr. Flagg personally put cold cloths and ice on his sister's frail frame. Then he found the ring. Being a bit wiser than his sister gave him credit for, he immediately figured out what was going on. She had damned eloped with some Irish bastard! Well, his friends in Charleston would soon take care of the bastard. Surely a new ship needed some extra ballast or someone needed some fill dirt for a foundation. In a white-hot fury, spurred by the dissolution of his plans, Dr. Flagg torn the chain from his sister's pallid neck and threw the ring out the open window, into the marsh beyond. Alice had enough awareness left to know that something had happened to her wedding band and she clawed at her neck, whimpering "My ring! My ring!" Soon afterwards, she lapsed into a coma and died a day or two later.

Over the next few years, slaves, Union soldiers, freedmen, and Yankee hunters all reported seeing the same thing. A beautiful blonde teenager in a shimmering high-necked white nightgown walking above the stagnant black water of the old rice fields turned to salt marsh frantically searching for something below her bare feet. When confronted, by a sentry, or night watchman or random passerby in their cups, she would bring her beautiful yet

ghastly pale face within inches of the witness and whisper…
"My ring, my ring! Please help me find my ring!" Of course,
the hearer, moved to tears by her pleading, would say yes and
turn away or glance down for a mere moment. When they
looked back up, she of course would be gone, as silent as she
had come.

Supposedly, in his old age, Dr. Flagg saw Alice again
when he was caught in the Sea Islands-hurricane of 1893. He
and his body servant were trying to return home from seeing
a patient when the storm, the biggest to hit the South
Carolina coast before Hurricane Hugo in 1989, came roaring
ashore. Dr. Flagg's servant lashed them both to a tree to ride
the storm out. The servant died but the doctor survived and
said that all of his deceased relatives came see him in his hour
of need. He said that Alice forgave him for losing her ring.

Of course, my girlfriend Alice is best known for the
ritual at her grave. It's over at All Saints Episcopal Church
off Highway 17. Yes, the church is still active, so for once
have some respect and don't bother folks on Sunday. If you
have to act like you have no home training, blame somebody
else, because I've done told all y'all. At any rate, ladies, this
one is for you. Now, I'd advise you use a dollar store ring
and not the one your other half spent a couple of grand on
if you try this. But you walk around the grave thirteen times
and then shut your eye and hold your hand out and say

"Alice, I found your ring." You can't miss her plot. It's the slab marked Alice with the rut worn around it. After you perform the ritual, you'll notice your ring, regardless of how tightly it was fitted, sliding slowly down your finger. If you aren't quick, it will fall into the pile in the center of the slab. And we all know, you don't take stuff off a grave... otherwise bad things may happen.

On my last visit a few years back, my wife Rachel and my buddy Bill and his wife Susan stopped by to check on Alice one hot July Saturday afternoon. Both ladies tried the ring ritual, but since Rooster and I had made honest women of them both, it sadly didn't work. I wandered around the cemetery, letting the history flow through me, when I caught a blast of wisteria. Like I had walked by a perfume counter in a department store on Christmas Eve. I was in a cloud of it as big as I was. The cemetery isn't huge, and I asked if anybody else could smell anything and no one could. I wandered back over to Alice's grave to say farewell, still wrapped in wisteria when I felt fingers run through the little bit of hair above my collar. I spun around and my wife and our friends were already crossing the road back to the car. I merely said bye and floated back to the car.

At least somebody likes me...

Historic Brattonsville

Historic Brattonsville is well-known to most folks in York and surrounding counties in South Carolina. It is a living-history farm, site of the Battle of Huck's Defeat, and served as a set for part of the filming of the Mel Gibson film *The Patriot*. The site has been on the National Register of Historic Places since 1971.

The first of these is the old slave cemetery off Burkins Road. I will remind all y'all, especially those who might want to spice up their Halloween with some thrill-seeking, that trespassing and vandalism are crimes, not pranks. Anyone caught in a cemetery after dark without permission from the landowners deserves whatever penalty the law hands down. Please don't disturb the dead, treat them and their markers with the same respect you would treat them with if they were still living. Anyway, the old slave cemetery is the site of Watt's grave and that of his wife Polly. They are the only marked graves at the site. According to the website, Watt was the slave who warned Colonel Bratton that the Loyalists under Major Huck were approaching. People have reported seeing a shadowy figure slipping through the woods at dusk. People have reported a feeling of deep sadness at the site just before the figure is seen. I have been to the site at the "right time," but have not seen anything to prove or disprove the tale.

The second area that has been reported as possibly being haunted is the Blacksmith's shop. Just before closing, visitors have described hearing odd banging sounds, like metal on metal coming from the locked building. Lights in the windows have also been reported, even when the building is empty. I have not seen anything unusual on my visit, but I may have just not been lucky. Do let me know if you find anything curious on your next visit, won't you?

Old Rose Hotel/ Apartments

The Rose Apartments in downtown York is located in the heart of the historic district and is home to one of my best friends. Before I wrap up this series on haunted sites in western York County, let me fill in the history of the site. The hotel was built sometime before 1865 and first entered history as the site of an address to the citizens of what was then Yorkville by Confederate Secretary of War (and former US Vice President) General John C. Breckenridge in April 1865. Confederate President Jefferson Davis slept next door at the home of Dr. James Rufus Bratton, a former Confederate surgeon at the same time. In 1872, Dr. Bratton fled his home next door to London, Ontario, Canada in order to avoid arrest for his Klan activities. Among these were the murder of a Black militia officer named Jim

Williams. He was lynched outside his home near York by masked riders, among whom one was later identified as Dr. Bratton. The body was found wearing a placard, "Jim Williams on his big muster." The incident helped Colonel Merrill (mentioned below) begin to identify and arrest Klan members in the area. He was seized at night, bound and gagged by agents of the US Government and returned to Yorkville to stand trial. His friends in Yorkville paid his bond and in order to avoid an international incident, he was released afterwards. Dr. Bratton's story helped inspire the novel *The Clansman* by Thomas Dixon, which in turn inspired the film epic *Birth of a Nation*.

During Reconstruction and the turmoil it brought to York, the Rose was owned by W.E. Rose, a Radical Republican leader in the County. The hotel served as headquarters for US troops under Colonel Lewis Merrill in the early 1870s during the imposition of martial law in York and surrounding counties due to the activities of the original Ku Klux Klan. The Rose was widely regarded as the most upscale hotel in Yorkville during this period, but it was not used by the local Democrats for rallies due to the political affiliation of its owner.

The Rose Apartments are very nice and quiet, though the lack of an elevator makes moving a bit of a struggle to the upper floors. According to an elected official of the city of York, odd events have occurred in the building. According to what I have heard, furniture moves on its own and footsteps have been heard in empty hallways. The site is also home to apparitions of men in both blue and gray uniforms as well as a lady in an old-fashioned hoop skirt who darts around corners. Certainly, the stress felt by those who accompanied Jeff Davis on his flight from Richmond and the Federal garrison stationed there during the height of Radical Reconstruction, not to mention the stress the Bratton family had during that same period would have left a mark on the site. The constant coming and going of so many guests over the years may be another source of whatever haunts the site.

I have been in the building at different times of the day on different days and have not had any unusual experiences. The hardwood floors in the upper hallways certainly echo one's footsteps and I keep listening for the tap of high heels on them or the heavy tread of a footsore infantryman, not to mention the crinkle of crinoline. My friend is on standby, with instructions to call me any time she sees or hears anything odd. I keep hoping…

Dutchman on the Congaree

This tale was told to be by a fella I chatted with around a fire ring at a long-ago Palmetto State Hangers hammock hang at a location that escapes me due to the passage of time. Sadly, since we were both DEEP in our cups (or jars as it were), his name, like the boogaloo, has plumb escaped me. I've tweaked it a bit, but the basic story is supposedly the gospel truth and the guy swore he'd been a witness. I'm letting him narrate it.

The Congaree River is mighty creepy under optimal conditions, but man, when the mist hangs low, it will chill the hottest blood. I've hung my hammock at Congaree National Park many times over the years, and I expect I've hiked every square foot of the place, at least the ones dry enough to walk on and I've never not spent a large part of the time looking over my shoulder. Besides Swamp Girl, South Carolina's most famous vanishing hitchhiker wandering around the US 601 bridge over the river and thereabouts; pick her up if you get a chance; there's no shortage of high strangeness afoot. If it's not the pack of wild dogs no one's ever seen, but everyone has heard, tearing by the primitive camping area in the wee hours of a rainy fall morning or the driverless coach and four careening down an old logging road with no worry for what it hits, be it one of Detroit's biggest trucks or a lone hiker; it's the sunken barge that won't stay sunk roaming the river proper. Kayakers and paddlers have been known to make better time up river than down after encountering it. I've seen it and it's just unexplainable.

The story I heard from my former boyfriend is that back in the antebellum days, down at Motte's Ferry, the oldest and busiest ferry on the river south of Columbia, things could get awful congested, like I-77 on a fall Saturday Carolina plays at Williams-Brice. At any rate, one of the plantations had a barge coming up river with a full load of cotton bound for Columbia. It had a crew of six onboard and as often happens, they were running behind schedule because of a thick layer of fog blanketing the river from bank to bank up to the tops of the bluffs. The skipper decided to make up time by both poling and paddling up river at double time and damn any obstacles. Now, the skipper was partial to his wine and stayed in a bad way and worse mood all the time, but this day he made a fatal error. He called on the help of the Devil himself to help him make up time for the low price of his soul. Being an obliging kind of fellow, the Devil appeared just before Motte's Ferry and asked how he could help. "Clear this blasted fog!" shouted the cap'n, spooking the horses waiting on the ferry upstream. "No, sir," said the Devil quietly, "but I will do you a favor just as helpful, if you vow to uphold our bargain." "Anything! What's a soul if you can't feed the body around it?" said the cap'n. At this, the crew of slaves retreated from the skipper and his invisible friend and headed for the safety of the bow, fearing what would come next. The Devil smiled and looked into the bloodshot eyes of the skipper and said, "Why my good fellow, you are simply overloaded. Permit me to lighten your load and speed your way! Oh, and I'll be taking payment now. Too many defaulters lately to wait until journey's end."

With that, the captain and his crew all vanished in a flash of blood-red light. Despite being in earshot of the ferry, all anyone on shore knew was that the steady splashing of the oars and pole ceased and then a sudden flash of light appeared in the center of the channel. When the barge finally appeared out of the mist, it was running at a good clip upstream, but no one was on board. The barge was not seen again, and most folks think it had slipped its moorings and floated away and sunk somewhere around the next bend. The fact that it was headed upstream was just ignored.

Nowadays, if you are lucky enough to be on the river itself or on the bank on the anniversary of this sorrowful event, you may be lucky enough to see the sudden flash of red light in midstream, followed by the sudden appearance of an antebellum river barge in mid-channel bearing down on you if you are in a canoe or kayak. But, given that the anniversary is usually marked by the heaviest mist on the Congaree in the last year, you will likely just hear loud laughter followed by sobs, and then a sudden flash of red light. Most folks say those unlucky enough to see the actual barge die by the next anniversary. Now, I think that's just silly. On our first date, my husband Jim and I saw it coming back from Charleston Pride just last year about this time. Of course, Jim passed away suddenly about a month later after he told me, "Tom, that damned barge is coming to pick us up." But c'mon, morphine makes folks say the damnedest things. Now, let's get off this sand bar and start paddling...

Brown Mountain Lights

The Wiseman's View Overlook off the Blue Ridge Parkway is the nearest thing I have to a "honey hole" for any would-be ghost hunter… you know that spot where even a bad fisherman is basically guaranteed to catch at least one fish. I've been there roughly two dozen times and just about every time I've gone, I've seen something. Now, in the gathering twilight after you've finished your picnic, it ain't much to look at, scenery-wise. Just a small valley leading up to a little humpback ridge. But that unassuming ridge is where the magic happens… Brown Mountain…. My happy place.

The lights that appear over Brown Mountain have been seen even prior to settlement in the area by colonists in the mid-1700s. The Natives told William Byrd while he was in the area that the lights had appeared as long as they could remember. Even today, they appear just prior to dusk, mainly in early Spring and Fall. For me, waiting for that first flicker of orange, blue, yellow, or white to appear over the raggedy pines in the distance is worth an occasional bug bite and glaze of sunburn. The lights vary in appearance: a blue one will shoot up like a Roman candle, followed by a yellow blip over the tree line at the far end of the ridge, then a white flash back towards the center, continuing for anywhere from two or three minutes to ten. Now, a gentle reminder, since some of y'all are hellbent to turn everything into ghosties. That big flashing red light in the bottom corner of your field of vision AIN'T a ghost. It's a cell tower, so you can live-stream the spooky goodness to your homebody friends.

As far as the source of the lights, who knows. But there is always a story or six. The Natives claim that the lights are the result of a battle for hunting rights on Brown Mountain between the Cherokee and the Catawba tribes. Two Cherokee survived and only one Catawba, so the Cherokee won the fight. The lights are supposed to be the pine knot torches used by the sisters, wives, daughters, and mothers of the dead warriors, trying to identify their loved ones amongst the slaughter. I'll buy that tale for a dollar.

But Scotty Wiseman (where do I know that name from?), an area native, wrote a song called *The Legend of the Brown Mountain Light*. In his version, a "faithful ole slave" from Charleston carries a kerosene lantern seeking "the bones of his master who's long, long gone." The hunter apparently walked off a ledge on the mountain pursuing a deer and broke his neck. I don't buy this tale because any slave from Charleston brought that far north would bolt for the Ohio River as quick as his feet or mule would tote him. The need for freedom would overwhelm any lingering affection for his master, to my mind.

Speaking of lanterns, yet another version claims that the lights are the lantern of a father seeking his children, sent out during a cold snap to gather the last blackberries of the season. They got bewildered and walked off the same ledge that claimed our great white hunter. However, they starved to death rather than dying of broken necks. Likely enough I reckon.

Of course, some folks have to drag UFOs into the mix. Meanwhile, I can think of a metric ton of more likely spots to go see UFOs. Of course, some folks think Zack Bagans isn't full of shit so...

Hell, if I know which story suits... y'all are free to choose as you wish. All I know is that when I go, most folks see the lights and think it's cooler than hell. Except for my best buddy Bill. He don't wanna see anything weird like the lights, so he don't. I've gone as far as to grab his head, and yes he's grown, and turn it for him. Still he just don't see the damned things. But he's game enough to tag along, so I can't give him too much shit.

Of course, all the great tales don't suit the gubmit (that's government for those of you who ain't fluent in Hillbilly speak.). So they have to explain it for us and to us.

The first attempt came back in the 1890s. The United States Coast and Geodetic Survey did several surveys in the area. In their defense, I worked for a land surveyor when I was in college, and we did some water line work up towards Morganton and Brown Mountain. That country is Hella cob rough now to try to haul a fifty-pound pack, a twenty-pound wooden tripod, and a bush hook even with paved roads to get close. So, I admire the fellas who went up to do the work, but they just got it wrong.

Anyways, they decided that the lights were easily explained. They were simply the refraction of the reflection of the dangle of the angle of the kerosene headlamps of the locomotives hauling freight over the trestle over the French Broad River over at Old Fort, North Carolina. Makes sense I reckon, until the 1903 Pacolet River flood took out damned near everything from north of Asheville down to Columbia. Hell, it took out a three-story cotton mill in Clifton South Carolina some hundred and change miles from Brown

Mountain down to the dirt. Folks were finding iron cotton looms around Columbia for a year after that. Not to mention the bodies it left behind. Even with that, folks who lived on the high ground noticed that the lights still popped up at random, even with all the trestles gone. Strike one for the gubmint.

The next attempt came a bit later on. In the later 1920s, the North Carolina Department of Agriculture said," No, no, we got this all worked out." They explained it in small words even. All the lights on Brown Mountain are very simply swamp gas. Ya know, what happens in optimal conditions when you have leaf litter and such fall into standing water and rot, causing stuff to give off gases that seem to spark off in certain conditions. I'm fairly certain that the above explanation is as accurate and scientific as a four-year-old explaining how a TV works, but I tell ghost stories…

At any rate, I've seen swamp gas in the wild. It looks like either someone trying to light a wet lighter in a hurricane or like a lightning bug and lasts about as long. Oh, and it usually appears about a foot or two off the ground, not at treetop level. Not to mention the fact that Brown Mountain is solid limestone, which soaks up water. No standing water, no puddles, no swamp gas. Strike two, as it were.

The most recent attempt to "solve the mystery of the

Brown Mountain Lights" by a gubmint agency dates back to the early Fifties. After we dropped the atomic bomb on Japan in 1945 and started work on the hydrogen bomb, the gubmint set up the Atomic Energy Commission to run these projects and such. To build more and better bombs, the United States needed raw uranium and plutonium by the pound. So, if you wrote into the Commission, they'd send you a free Geiger Counter to go find these radioactive elements and likely even pay you for doing so. I mean, let's give kids valuable gadgets to go play with radiation. What could ever go wrong? But anyhoo, the Commission also scouted the Appalachians for larger amounts that were closer to the laboratory in Oak Ridge, Tennessee. Supposedly, they detected roughly a ton of uranium-238 at the heart of Brown Mountain and determined that the lights were the result of radiation sparking off in the atmosphere.

Did I miss the time we dropped the limestone bomb on Baghdad during one of the many wars we fought over there? Because the last time I checked, limestone ain't a fissionable material and is as about as radioactive as mud. So, strike three for the gubmint and to heck with them.

Of course, several professors have determined that the lights are simply reflections of headlights and taillights from traffic on Interstate Forty filtered through the haze and trees.

Maybe. If I know of anybody who lived in that part of the world who could tell me if the lights appeared after the devastation Hurricane Helene wrought, we'd settle that hash pretty quick. All I know is that if you go up to the Wiseman's View Overlook off the Blue Ridge Parkway just before dusk on a clear Fall or Spring day, you'll likely see the lights and I doubt that at that moment you'll care what they "actually" are. You'll just sit there with a shit-eating grin on your face knowing you just experienced something unexplained.

Found Out About This One from a Man What Knows...

In my decades of hammock camping with my buddy Bill (aka Rooster: I'm Pudden), I've met some truly awesome folks. A boatload of these folks have become dear and deeply beloved friends, even at a distance. One of those folks is a guy named John Rammel, who makes damn fine hammocks, quilts, and other gear for those of us with more sense that to try to sleep on the ground (at my age, I'd just have to live there... on my back like a cartoon turtle... while everything hurts). John runs Trailheadz Hammocks up in Bellbrook Ohio. A few of my hammock peeps had been to an informal hang on his farm just outside Bellbrook and told me tales of epic fire rings, great food, and better moonshine. Well, I of course sat up like a toddler offered free candy and said when's the next one and they told me it was that Labor Day weekend which gave me like three weeks to get time off work and gird my loins for the looming eight-hour drive. Now, I wasn't dreading the ride per se, but I did know that I would pay a steep price for doing it. Way back in the before times, when I was still young, before any of y'all were even thought of, I was a driving fool (as opposed to the plain vanilla fool I am now.) Drive ten hours in a day to do a fandom con up in Louisville, Kentucky? Absol-damn-lutely. Run to Charleston from Charlotte for dessert on a random Saturday? Hells yeah! Load 'em up. Now? Drive four hours to Roanoke Virginia for a fandom con? Ok, I'll have to take the next Monday off and bring the big jug of Tylenol. Drive anywhere over an hour away on the weekend? Only on Saturday... a boy has to recuperate for the work week. But for the prospect of seeing folks I haven't seen in a minute, eating good in the woods, sleeping under the stars, and maybe getting my drinky drink on too? Yeah, I'd suck it up. So, when the appointed Friday arrived, away I went at five a.m. to drive through the mountains to finally tell my unique lies on the other side of the Ohio River... yes, kids, Pudden was invadin' the North, lol. And for you Rooster boosters, he made the next trip up the next Spring.

After hitting every rest area between my house in Chester and said river, I finally made it to John's place about five o'clock maybe four thirty. When I pulled up, there was about a fifty-foot hill looming over me to the actual camping area. Just as my aching knees began to bitch like it was their only function, here came my buddy Chris Gerken, aka Pickl, with a four-wheeler and a paper spit cup. On seeing my confusion, he informed me that he knew I'd be wore out and wanted to spare me the wear and tear, and that the cup was well worth it. And yes, it was. Real moonshine, good high proof and you could taste the limestone and copper in it. Thankfully, I had already lit my cigarette. On my arrival at the top of the hill, several other familiar faces descended on me for hugs, among others: Shannon Harris from Kentucky and my buddy Cajun aka Barry Garibaldi. John came up and introduced himself with a bit larger paper cup in hand and told me that it was tradition to do a shot of good shine when a new arrival first appeared and after they came back from setting up their gear. Of course, I had to be sociable, and I conformed to the custom. Now, lest you think all we drank was moonshine, you wouldn't be far off. But we did have a water cooler, a coke cooler, a beer cooler, a picnic table full of top shelf booze, AND a picnic table full of the best offerings from Sugarlands Shine to boot. I will confess that the six gallons of shine were all gone when I left Sunday morning. John also informed me and the other twenty odd folks there, that he knew a guy but that unlike the chili, he himself didn't make the corn squeezins. When I came back up, I noticed the fire ring… twenty feet wide and across with what appeared to be a whole tree burning away, despite the seventy-degree weather. John explained that he was clearing off some storm damage and downed trees. I gave him a signed copy of *Civil War Ghosts of South Carolina* and a copy of one of Alexandra Christian's (Rachel's) finest too… and he gave me two books of ghost lore from Ohio.

After an amazing supper, complete with real gumbo made by Cajun and wild game chili, John made me an offer I'd never had extended to me in some two decades of storytelling… a guided tour of spooky sites around Bellbrook. The man knew his stuff and was and is excellent company. One of the spots he showed is discussed below. Needless to say, I've been back once and am hoping to get back soon, once real-life stops being a bother as always…. Besides, how often does one get to tell spooky lies in front of a blazing TREE with fifteen-foot flames behind you?

The ghost of a woman who had Bellbrook's mayor's illegitimate child is said to haunt the banks of the creek. She jumped into it with her child after she was abandoned by the mayor. Witnesses have reported seeing her walking along the banks, singing to her child. The activity is said to increase during the month of June.

The small, unassuming town of Bellbrook, located near Dayton, has more than its share of ghostly legends and stories. Indeed, some refer to the area as "Ohio's Sleepy Hollow." In particular, the area of the town near Magee Park is alleged to be home to several ghosts.

The first spirit may be the one responsible for Bellbrook acquiring the "Sleepy Hollow" moniker. Legend has it that the headless ghost of a man named James Buckley wanders the area along Little Sugar Creek where his sawmill once stood.

Buckley lived in a small cabin along the creek and also operated a sawmill on the property. Over the course of time, Buckley managed to transform his small operation into a successful enterprise. In fact, he became one of the wealthiest men in the town, making him an easy target for thieves.

One night, Buckley's home was broken into and robbed. When authorities arrived, they found the headless body of James Buckley lying outside. Despite an investigation, the murder was never solved... and his head was never found.

While the cabin still stood, it was avoided by locals as it was alleged to be haunted. The few people who were brave enough to venture near the house reported being confronted by a headless ghost, his arms outstretched to them as if

69

pleading for help. One couple who rented the old cabin claimed to have sighted James Buckley standing at the front door, his ghostly head tucked under his arm.

Today, nothing remains of Buckley's cabin or his sawmill. But there are those that claim his headless ghost still wanders the property, imploring anyone who sees him for help.

Another ghost rumored to haunt Little Sugar Creek is that of a young suicide victim from the late 1800s. It is said that this young woman was involved in an illicit affair with a prominent politician, perhaps the Mayor of Bellbrook. The secret relationship went from bad to worse when the woman became pregnant.

Once the child was born, the woman found herself unable to support it. With nowhere else to turn, she went to the politician's home and begged for help. He refused to have anything to do with the woman or the child and had them removed from the property. Despondent, the young woman walked with her child to a bridge overlooking Little Sugar Creek. It is reported that she stood there for a while, softly singing to the bundle in her arms. Then she plunged into the dark water below. Her body was recovered several days later. She was still tightly clutching a bundle of cloth in her arms, but the child was gone.

Today, people have reported seeing the ghostly apparition of a woman walking slowly along the banks of Little Sugar Creek. She is most often sighted on foggy nights in June. Many also state that she appears to be singing softly to a bundle she carries in her arms.

Happy Hound of Goshen

The Happy Hound is one of the better-known tales from the Upcountry of South Carolina. The story dates back to the 1840s. The Hound is usually seen between Whitmire and Cross Anchor near and along the Old Buncombe Road, which was one of the main routes from Charleston and Asheville and points north. As such, it was heavily used by tradesmen, statesmen, and salesmen.

Our story commences with a peddler returning to his home north of Spartanburg from a very successful month of sales in Charleston. He got waylaid by one of South Carolina's famed summer storms and stopped to have a drink or two and some supper at a now long-forgotten tavern near Maybinton Crossroads. He and his hound settled into a chair with a mug of the best "corn squeezins" Union County had to offer and a plate of fried squirrel. The mug was a bit small, so he had two or three more. The deeper he got in his cups, the more he flashed his ready cash from his recent trip to impress the waitress and all that. Some of the local gentry definitely took notice and tracked him like a kid watching Santa's path on NORAD.

After about four mugs of corn juice, our newly flush peddler had to go visit the outhouse behind the inn just before dark. Of course, the white hound padded along behind, to do the same and generally investigate a new spot. About six gentlemen followed at a discreet distance and met him as he was leaving. They did not want to discuss the weather or local politics. They beat the peddler to death and then rolled his body down the bank behind the outhouse. The hound did all he could to defend his drunken owner, but stout sticks overcame ravening jaws and the hound fell unconscious beside his master. After the assailants headed home to nurse their wounds and the passage of about an hour, the absence of the peddler was noticed, due to his unpaid bill, and the innkeeper found the remains of the man's shirt in front of the empty outhouse and observed the marks in the mud of the struggle and where the body had been tossed. A general alarm was raised, of course, but all of the assailants were fairly well-known and well-off in the rural community, so no one was ever arrested for the murder. A

Dr. Douglass was summoned from his house across from the tavern, but not even medical training would help. The coroner returned a verdict of death by misadventure and buried the man in an unmarked grave in Goshen churchyard. Mankind did not attempt to avenge the hound's master, so he would do it. The hound settled down to guard his master's grave and threw himself at every man who was involved in the attack much to their upset. After two weeks of refusing food and water, the hound finally died on top of the grave and was then buried with him.

After the death of the hound, strange things started to happen in the vicinity of the tavern. Two of the half dozen assailants died suddenly when a white shape dashed out of the woods and ran between the legs of their horses. Two of the elder members of the gang died dueling each other over the virtue of one of the waitresses at the tavern. Her death the next week giving birth to one of their illegitimate children proved that the offended party was in the right, as it were. The fifth man died of heatstroke while overseeing his slaves. They reported that a great white hound, as tall as a man's waist, stood between their unfortunate master and the water jug, leaping at his throat every time he reached for it. The sixth, well, we'll discuss him in a bit, maybe. He lived to a decent age, but even reaching the heights of his profession turned out to be fool's gold.

As time passed, the peddler's murder faded from memory, but the hound remained. Reports of a giant hound keeping pace with coaches at full run on dark nights and walking THROUGH pines alongside nighttime walkers were common for the next century and more. The hound was seen on several occasions to vanish outside the wrought-iron gates of the Douglass farm, but everyone knew he'd soon return.

Fast-forward a century or so and I've just nailed an interview for the park ranger gig at Rose Hill State Historic Site. Since it is just up the road from Goshen Hill and Maybinton Road, I decided to try and pay a visit to the Happy Hound. I turned down Maybinton about a half hour before dark. After crossing State Highway 34, I decided to circle back up to State 72 and to head on back to the house. Roughly a mile from 34, I glanced into the pine woods next to the road and saw a flash of white. It looked to be about four feet off the ground and seemed to be headed my way at a good clip. My first thought is that was a deer on a suicide mission, but it got to the edge of the tree line and I saw it was a white hound. I cackled like a hen laying a dozen eggs at once. I slowed down to about forty-five and the dog kept pace. When I sped back up to sixty, he did the same. Then he jumped onto the asphalt behind me and gave chase. After about a half mile, I saw the twin red brick pillars of the old wrought-iron gate to the former Douglass plantation just ahead. I recollected that the dog was supposed to vanish into the gate, so I whipped my Chevy Corsica into the patch of gravel just in front of the posts and waited. Sure enough, the hound leapt over the hood of my car when it reached the spot the old gate would have occupied, it vanished, telescoping down to nothing, like an antenna on one of Detroit's land yachts from the 70s.

Rose Hill

Now, if you've read my book *Civil War Ghosts of South Carolina*, you know, despite my funny accent, that I ain't exactly a huge fan of Lost Cause bullshit. The Civil War was fought over slavery. The South had been picking the fight for thirty years before Lincoln's election. The South deserved to lose the war and Reconstruction should have lasted another twenty years at least. Now having said that, it does mean that some major parts of American history either happened or had their seeds planted within a few hours' drive of me.

One of those things was the fact that the man who called the Secession Convention for South Carolina after Lincoln won the presidency lived about forty-five minutes via back roads from my back door. Willian Henry Gist was a state representative and senator from Union District (now County) for some fifteen years and served as Lieutenant Governor of South Carolina prior to being elected Governor in 1858. While he was in the South Carolina General Assembly and as Governor, he strongly supported the institution of Black slavery, as well as reopening the trans-Atlantic slave trade! A real class act... Anyway, after Lincoln's election, he conspired with the Governors of Florida (of course) and Mississippi (I'm stunned) for South Carolina to leave the Union, followed the other two states and then others. Rose Hill did serve as the Governor's Mansion during his tenure. After the state left the Union, and Gist proudly signed the Ordinance of Secession, he served on the Executive Council for the first two years of the War. He managed to get a pardon at the end of the war and managed to "suffer" through Reconstruction and African-American rule of South Carolina before he died in 1874. Now, on to why y'all are here, the ghosts...

The area around Rose Hill State Historic Site itself has its own share of legends. One story concerns mysterious lights that appear in the nearby woods just after dawn. Hunters claim that the light resembles a man on horseback carrying a lantern. Those who have seen the light believe it is Governor Gist, still making his morning rounds. Since legend has it that his horse was buried next to him, it is possible that this figure is him and I can believe that he would still be interested in the state of affairs at his former home.

A few years back, I decided to take advantage of my

blushing bride's trip to the movies and decided to spend a Fall afternoon at Rose Hill. I did the house tour for the fifth or sixth time and wandered the grounds. Just before dark, I decided to chance aching knees and did the nature trail. It was easy walking if a bit unmaintained. It went to the Tyger River, a river I am intimately familiar with from my days growing up in Lyman splashing in and wondering around the Middle Tyger branch of said river. As I smoked a cigarette and drained my water bottle, I glanced up the near bank and saw a bluish light about five hundred yards or so upstream. Now, I was only a smidgen tired, not slobber knocker exhausted and there were some tree branches kinda in the way. But I just stood there and watched for about ten seconds, trying to process exactly what the hell it was… when it began to drift towards me real slow, like someone was trying to process what the hell I was doing there. I took that as my cue to get the flying fuck out of Dodge as it were and head back up the trail to my car. Besides, I was getting a bit hungry.

There is another story concerning the Gist family and the area around Rose Hill. Prior to the Civil War, one of Governor's Gist's daughters and a slave companion were out berry picking near what is now Sardis Road. A carriage came along and, for whatever reason, the horses were spooked. The daughter dove into the woods unharmed, but the slave girl was killed. Drivers along that road have reported seeing the two girls along the roadside, then witnessing the white child dive into the woods while the black girl vanishes just before the oncoming car plows into her. I haven't seen the ladies yet, despite multiple trips to Rose Hill over the years. But one of these days...

Other stories concerning the area around Rose Hill include the troop of Confederate cavalry that has been seen on the road leading past the main house and in the surrounding woods but only heard on the gravel drive in front of the house and never seen. Sadly, I've not met these fellows yet, visible or not, but I reckon it just means I have to keep going back.

And that don't even cover the old Crybaby Bridge at the bottom of the hill. Sadly, it is now closed to vehicle traffic, but it was still there on my last visit besides the new bridge over the creek coming in from Union.

During a visit as part of a much longer road trip to take pictures for *Civil War Ghosts of South Carolina*, my brother-in-law, Justin Glanville (aka the Aussie-in-law) and I took some photos of the exterior of the main house and inside the reconstructed outbuildings. In the outdoor kitchen, he reported the "face-finder" on his digital camera kept zooming in at a spot in the lower right of the photo just above the floor. Nothing appeared on any of the four shots he took, not even an orb. Just another day chasing ghosts...

The Gray Man

The Gray Man of Pawleys Island is probably the best-known ghost in South Carolina, and his tale is oft-told. He has appeared since 1822. Lucky tourists and residents of Pawleys have reported either seeing a figure dressed in gray on the beach or being approached by him just before a major tropical storm passes over. Those lucky enough to encounter him come through the storm unharmed or with minimal damage to their property. However, the living identity of the Gray Man has eluded researchers for decades,

Although sightings have been reported before major storms in 1822 (a hurricane that killed three hundred), 1893 (the Sea Island Hurricane that killed fifteen hundred people), 1954 (Hurricane Hazel, at least six hundred dead) and 1989 (Hurricane Hugo, a hundred and seven dead). Here are the three candidates:

First, we have the first settler and namesake of the island Percival Pawley. His sons inherited his large land grant after his death about 1748. However, though his sons were very civic minded, sponsoring Chapels of Ease and buying town lots in Georgetown, there is little record Percival ever actually set foot on his land grant as anything more than an investment.

Secondly, we have the unnamed returning lover of an equally anonymous island lass from a clash with the Indians. He rode on horseback up the coast from Georgetown to Pawleys Island. In his haste he took a shortcut through the marsh behind the dunes and horse and rider both tumbled into quicksand to their doom. The heartbroken young lady paced the beach for weeks seeking news of her love. Accounts vary on whether the couple was engaged or already married. After a few months, rumors of a large storm reached Pawleys. The girl's father decided not to evacuate due to some pressing business. A day or two before landfall while she was on the beach, the young lady saw her love approach on foot. He warned to her and her family to leave the island right away and immediately vanished. Upon hearing the story, the girl and her parents fled inland and avoided a horrible storm with no damage to their property. The storm he reputedly saved her and hers from was the 1822 hurricane.

Another version of this story makes the man an

unsuitable suitor for the daughter of a major rice planter from Charleston who had been sent away to Europe. The girl was told her lover had been killed in a duel and she then married her father's choice of husband. She and her husband honeymooned at Pawleys. The distraught young lover had turned to the sea to heal his broken heart and by some uncanny stroke of luck was shipwrecked off Pawleys Island and rescued by a servant of the husband. Learning the identity of his nurse, the man fled inland and died of an undetermined fever. The next year, he returned from the grave to warn his lover to flee her Pawleys Island retreat just before a storm hit, vanishing before the eyes of both her and her husband.

The final candidate for being the most famous ghost is South Carolina is Plowden Charles Jeannerette Weston, Lieutenant Governor of South Carolina under Milledge Luke Bonham and Company commander of the Georgetown Rifle Guards, a home guard unit. He was also the builder of the Pelican Inn, which is also haunted. Plowden Weston was also the owner of Hagley Plantation, which we will visit shortly and yeah, I think he still wanders there too.

Mr. Weston was also a historian and powerful orator. His love for the island was only rivaled by his love for his wife Emily or for his home Hagley. The biggest difficulty with naming Plowden Weston as the Gray Man is the fact that the first reported appearance was in 1822 when Plowden was just two years old. However, I am of the firm opinion that the 1822 Gray Man was the unnamed dead lover lost to quicksand and that the other sightings are of Plowden Weston.

The Pelican Inn is also haunted by a Lady in Gray, who some witnesses think is Emily Plowden. She appears in a dress of gray gingham with pearl buttons and a white apron. She has been seen in the kitchen, and on the staircase going towards the bedrooms. Other witnesses think she could be a cousin of Emily and Plowden Weston, Mrs. William Mazyck, who inherited the Pelican Inn after the deaths of the Westons.

The other ghosts reported at the Pelican Inn are two Boston Terriers that have been seen playing in the surf and on the beach in front of the house at dusk, only to vanish after a few seconds, leaving just tracks in the sand.

Hagley Landing

Hagley Landing is located on the Waccamaw River and is on property that once made up Hagley Plantation, the pride and joy of Plowden C.J. Weston mentioned above in connection with the legend of the Gray Man of Pawleys Island. Plowden Weston could well being doing **double duty**, haunting two of his homes and protecting the island he loved. I doubt it, but then I can be a bit of a hopeless romantic. However. The sad tale that follows is something that would make Margaret Mitchell or Eudora Welty proud, but that I doubt any self-respecting editor would allow to see print.

The story begins as so many do, with a wedding towards the end of the Civil War. The wedding was held at the plantation chapel, now sadly dismantled and scattered to the ends of Georgetown County, but the stained-glass windows did survive and were given to Prince George Winyah Episcopal Church in Georgetown. A young bride married a dashing young swain and all was happiness. The wedding party retired to the landing to head off on their honeymoon and to accept the congratulations of the gathered throng. Until a Confederate soldier in a ragged uniform rode up on a horse worn past all endurance and confronted the bride. She broke down, crying that she thought the soldier had been killed in battle. The soldier then promised not to interfere with the couple's happiness and leapt from the dock into the river, which was rapidly flowing out with the tide. The bride and groom then followed, one after the other as their guests watched in shock.

The first account of the haunting at Hagley dates from 1918 with a young man, waiting for his girlfriend to arrive via motor launch from Georgetown so they could attend a party on Pawleys Island. He saw the three unhappy suicides strolling down the road towards the landing. When he tried to speak, all three faded away as suddenly as they appeared. There have been reports of the figures being seen since, always on dark and misty nights.

The former Hagley Plantation is now a subdivision, and the old landing is now a public boat dock for accessing the Waccamaw River, but the road leading to it is well-paved. I have sat there several times when conditions were right, but I have not been lucky... yet.

Part Two:

Falsehoods for Fandom

GHOST OF A CHANCE

Some ghosts enlighten.

Some ghosts frighten.

Some ghosts entertain.

Some ghosts only in dreams remain.

Some ghosts charm.

Some ghosts alarm.

Some ghosts bring out fears,

While some ghosts reduce us to tears.

Some ghosts haunt us like memories

Returning when least bidden to do so.

Some ghosts vanish when exposed

As frauds, fakes, or rip-off schemes.

Are your ghosts real-

Or merely the flickers of

A fading flame in a distant, shattered mirror?

The Tanning Yard

One of the biggest draws for telling this story is, well, folks of all ages seem to enjoy hearing about grown men making fools for themselves. Now, in my limited defense, I was a teenager, so my fool quotient was rather higher back in those ancient days. I mean, the Lord looks out for fools and little children, and I wasn't little, so... I also love this story because it was one of the things that really sank the hook in on the whole ghost story/paranormal investigation thing.

Back in the long ago late 1980s, I was a small-town high school junior with devious friends, too much free time, and a mind that wandered towards all things ghostly. At any rate, one fall Sunday night after church, a bunch of us were sitting at the local Ryan's Steakhouse shooting the bull and making the owner cry by eating the buffet bare when some bright spark said those immortal words... "Y'all wanna see a ghost girl?"

Well, being in the death grip of puberty, he had every mother's son of us at girl. The ghost was just a bonus. All of a sudden, he had two dozen eyes locked on him. Of course, it was all complete and utter bullshit. But we didn't know that then and wouldn't have given a pluperfect damn if we had.

The story is rather pitiful in the daylight. Back in the 1970s, a group of Satanists decided to do a ritual that involved sacrificing female virgins from every high school in Spartanburg County South Carolina. Yup, all nine of them. That should have told us right there it was pure uncut bullshit, but we were young. One of the young ladies escaped, wearing only a flimsy white night gown and took off down the creek at a full sprint. Of course, she slipped on the rocks, fell, and broke her neck. The Satanists got caught and that was that. Of course, it wasn't. The dead girl came back every night and would float down the creek to your car if you parked on the rickety wooden bridge over Falling Creek and honked three times. Or flashed your bright lights three times. Or something... he wasn't sure. We decided we'd go check it out and do both, just in case. I mean, if one worked, two was a guarantee, right? So, we all got sweet teas to go and piled into somebody's Ford Ranger. Yup, a dozen teen boys in a pickup the size of a couch... nothing bad would happen, right?

Hoo boy, just wait. After about three wrong turns...
"it's a LEFT off Highway 29, you dumbass! No, your other
left! You HAVE been here before, right? SHUT UP! It was
daylight when I was here last. Did you cross the tracks or
not? Well, shit, now we have to turn around." Yeah, we were
a regular Algonquin Round Table. Of course this was filtered
through a mixtape featuring Al B. Sure, 2 Live Crew, The
Police, Hank Williams Junior, Def Leppard, and Lord knows
what else. And the wind noise that buffets you sitting on the
tailgate of an overcrowded pickup. At least it wasn't freezing.

After about twenty minutes of touring the lowlights of
the west side of Spartanburg, we finally made the turn down
Falling Creek Road. Many comments were made about the
demons lurking in the kudzu and the potentially inbred
rednecks we'd meet in the back of beyond. Yeah, I know,
mill hill kids ripping on rednecks... go figger.

After about five minutes of bouncing down a paved
road that was more potholes and gravel than pavement, we
finally got to the bridge. It was a flat wooden bridge with no
guardrails about twenty feet long and wide enough for one
car at a time, maybe. About a tenth of a mile up the creek, a
high railroad trestle loomed. I knew it was on the main line
between Atlanta and Charlotte, just like the ones I used to
ride bikes across and run foot races on. I never claimed to

have a lick of common sense.

My scrawny self was perched on the tailgate of the pickup, right at dead center. On one side was a guy who played tackle on the offensive line who was a junior like me and on the other was a freshman not much bigger than I was. Well, after some hollering between us and the driver, the fun started. The headlights flashed and then three blasts of the horn drowned out the gurgle of the creek and the chorus of tree frogs. Every one of us swung our heads upstream towards the one puny streetlight about a half mile away. Then we heard it. The voice of a very, very pissed off woman, screaming about damn kids and waking people up and several unflattering things about our parentage and such. As she got closer, we could see she was at least in a nightgown, flannel, but still. Then we heard the mind-focusing noise of two shells being racked into a shotgun. Well, that sealed it. The guy on my left threw his arms out and shouted "Go! Go! I'm too pretty to die!" When he threw his arms out, he knocked me off the tailgate and onto my flat ass. I swear I felt the wood on the bridge bounce. As I tried to jump up and climb back into the truck, the driver got the hint just as the first barrel went off. And away he sped. Now, I'm nobody's fool and I realized that the nice lady with the shotgun wasn't looking for a civil chat. So I jumped into the creek and hid under the bridge, silently cussing out each and every jackass in that long gone Ranger. The woman emerged on to the road between the bridge and the trestle. I heard every obscenity she muttered and silently prayed she would glance my direction. After what seemed like an hour, she stomped off back to her house. After what seemed like another hour, my buddy came back around to the bridge, where I stood sopping wet and extremely pissed off. I got into the cab and cussed him and his all the way back to Lyman. I hope I ruined those cloth seats. For some reason, we didn't stay in touch after graduation.

The Powell Theater/Chester Little Theater

What follows seems to be the lie I tell the most and seems to be the one folks like best, especially kids. I'm going to change this up just a smidgen and give you some background and then give you the told version.

According to some older citizens of Chester, the area where the Little Theater is now was the site of the public gallows as far back as the 1780s. However, the gallows have also been reputedly located on Henry Woods Drive and at the first old jail, now a law office. The more likely explanation for the haunting of the Chester Little Theater dates from the early 1930s. In July 1932, the Bell family owned and operated the Chester Telephone Company. These Bells were not related by blood to Alexander Graham Bell: the common name is just a happy accident of history. The long-distance operators for the phone company were located at 109 Wylie Street, now the Chester ARP Church offices. Next door to them was the City (now known as the Powell) Theater at 103 Wylie. The operators were on the second floor of the telephone company building.

On July 14, 1932, young Daniel Bell was preparing to take a shower and struck a match to light a lamp in a basement on Wylie Street. Apparently, the shower was provided for employees to clean up if they got dirty during the workday. The Chester Reporter newspaper account dated July 18, 1932, states that Mr. Bell was in the telephone company basement when he struck this fatal match, setting alight some escaping gas and causing the boiler to explode. Despite being severely burned and nude, Mr. Bell gave no thought to his own welfare, but darted upstairs to warn the female operators of the danger, getting the three that were on duty out of the building with only minor injuries. Mr. Bell died of his wounds on Saturday the 16th of July, 1932.

However, the most commonly told version of the story places Mr. Bell and his bath next door in the basement of

Barron's Funeral Home. His personal bravery cannot be discounted, though, as regardless of where he was bathing, he did save the lives of the three ladies at work for his family's firm. The boiler explosion was blamed on a faulty pilot light and phone service was quickly reconnected.

Odd events have occurred at the Chester ARP Church offices in the old Bell Annex at 109 Wylie Street since the church acquired it in 1981. Linda Tinker, the former church secretary, told me that she has heard male voices and footsteps upstairs at odd hours and that once a former pastor told her to stop talking so loudly, as he was on the phone. She was outside smoking at the time. She has also heard footsteps on the steps leading to the second floor as well. When I went to examine the area, I heard no one upstairs but I did feel a breeze while looking around upstairs, as if I had been passed by someone in a hurry. Speculation is that the hauntings here are related to the death of Dan Bell.

Despite the activity at the other two sites on Wylie Street, the real hot spot is the old Powell Theater building at 103 Wylie Street, now home to the Chester Little Theater. The old Dreamland/Powell/ Little Theater holds a special place in my heart for several reasons. It's one of the most haunted sites I've ever dealt with. All of my in-laws and loads of my friends have acted or worked backstage at multiple plays over the years. My wife and I actually acted together a few times. Not bad for a guy who was so shy and had such an awful speech impediment that doing that in high school or even college would have made me weep, cower, and cuss at the very mention of the prospect. Sadly, the building now sits empty, unsafe for multiple reasons. But one of these days, I'll back in to "play."

More than six different ghosts have made their presences felt in the building over the years. The most recent haunt to appear is the ghost of a woman found stuffed into a dumpster in the alley at the rear of the backstage area in the early 1980s. Terry Cameron was inside the building sewing costumes when she heard a thump on the wall behind her. Looking out into the alley, she saw no one and returned to work. The next morning, the body was found and no one has yet identified it. Naturally, Terry does not volunteer to work in the building alone now. Several years after the murder, a bathroom for actors and others backstage was built just inside the building from where the body was found. This bathroom has since been notorious for cold spots and for faucets inexplicably turning on and off. There have been bangs and thumps heard on the outside wall as well. When the area is checked, no evidence is ever found of any recent human activity.

The stage at the Little Theater is also a hot spot for activity. Facing the stage, the area in the wings on the front right is known as "Norm's spot." Norm was a prop handler who always stood in the same spot just off stage in the wings. After his suicide, which did not happen at the theater, the odd happenings in the area began. Actors have been known to trip here for no reason; props have constantly been misplaced; and cold spots have been reported. As annoying as these can be, they are nothing compared to the shock that Terry Cameron and Becky White got one night after a rehearsal. They were going up the aisle when a flicker from the stage caught their eyes. Having no idea where the light came from, they turned and saw two cylinders of light on the stage moving back and forth. After calmly watching for about a minute, both ladies felt goose bumps and hurriedly left the building. The former projection booth was not yet enclosed at the time of this incident, but the movement of the cylinders seems to eliminate any reflection as the source.

To end our tour of the stage area, let's look at two cases of auditory manifestation. Both cases happened during rehearsals, one during *Man of La Mancha*. The cast was using a tape recording to fix the lyrics in their mind, focusing on. "The Psalm" that night. Up to that point, all had gone as expected. But when Glinda Price Coleman cued up that particular song (after the tape had been left onstage overnight), it played back in reverse. No other songs were the least bit out of the ordinary. After rehearsal, Mrs. Price Coleman played the tape in her car while going home, and the playback was normal on every track, even "The Psalm."

The second odd auditory event happened during a dress rehearsal for *All Because of Agatha*. The stage manager, Mrs. Alice Addison, was using a headset to communicate from backstage to the lighting booth. Halfway through Act 1, Mrs. Addison came on stage as white as a ghost and shaking. She insisted that everyone listen to her headset. Those present heard a baby crying at the top of its lungs. There was not a baby present at the time and when the headset was cut off, no crying was heard. Everyone laughed it off as merely interference from a nearby baby monitor until the group realized that the nearest house was about a quarter of a mile away.

Voices, footsteps, creaks and other noises have disturbed many rehearsals. But the stage area is not the only part of the theater where odd events have occurred. Both the stage and the seating areas have attracted large numbers of visible orbs. Orbs are typically visible only in photographs, but are usually accompanied by cold spots or other physical manifestations. During my visits to the theater in the last year, I have taken many photographs - some in which orbs are present. Since the Chester Little Theater (and the whole side of Wylie Street, for that matter) is seemingly infested with orbs, let me address these problematic manifestations here. Most photographs of many stationary orbs are, in all likelihood, simply dust particles or bugs reflecting the light from a camera flash. Photographs with movement or color change, or single, well-defined orbs, are more likely to be manifestations of a ghost of some kind.

In one photograph I took, an orb was present; in my second shot less than five seconds later, the orb was gone. At the time of my first photo, Al Pratt, a veteran actor and middle school history teacher who was there with me during this particular hunt, was describing the presence of an older white woman just outside his reach. Shortly after the second photo was taken, Mr. Pratt reported that the lady was gone. With your back to the stage, the area where he saw the image is in the rear of the seating area on your left.

Upstairs in the set storage area curious things have appeared in the windows facing Wylie Street. Nikki Bramlett, a longtime actor and director at the theater, saw a white woman in her sixties staring down at the street from the window. One photograph I took of the exterior of the building showed an orb in this window. This occurred in February of 2005 during rehearsals for the show *Five Women*

Wearing the Same Dress. This figure, sighted by Ms. Bramlett and possibly caught by my camera, may be the same woman who beckoned to me from the top of the lobby stairs while I was waiting for the intermission of *My Three Angels*. Sadly, I have no idea what she wanted, as discretion overcame my usual impulsiveness and I declined her invitation. Shortly after her appearance, one of the stagehands came up and drafted me into filling in for a sick actor. He did not see the lady or notice how pale I was. Her identity remains unknown; I have no information on any older woman coming to any sort of harm on the site. Most folks guess that she may have been linked to an antique bed stored upstairs instead of the building proper.

Now, to the told version. I do work in some of the events mentioned above, but my focus is usually on the cast bathroom backstage, the old projection booth, and the entrance from the alley up to the balcony, especially the stairwell.

During rehearsals for the play *The Weir* (the last show held at the Powell by the Chester Little Theater), I decided not to drive home in my makeup since I looked like I had tried and failed to pull off booger drag. So, into the backstage bathroom I went. Ladies, I don't know how y'all can stand to wear makeup, and I especially don't get how y'all can take it off. Being uneducated in the process, I popped the hook and eye lock on the door and cut light on with the pull cord and commenced. I put hot water all over my face and then cold cream and went to town scrubbing. About the time I got the base layer off, the light went off and yes, I heard the pull cord click behind me. As I groped for the chain with makeup and cold cream running into my eyes, the sink cut off. Behind me. With my hands in the air. So, I cussed louder and finally wiped most of the stuff out of my now burning eyes. I found the door and flipped the hook out... And the damned door wouldn't pull open. Now, back then I was in decent shape and opening a pull door hadn't been an issue. After what seemed like fifteen minutes, the door flew open and I burst into the backstage area in full rant. I mean full on redneck with an ax to grind with language to match. My fellow cast mates and the crew looked at me like I had live lobsters on my face. Of course, no one had seen me go into the bathroom, so there was no reason for anyone to prank me. I wrote it off as the lady from the dumpster making her presence felt.

The old projection booth is another hot spot, as it were. I've had three experiences in the room, but one was just funny as Hell. The first is mentioned above when I heard the steady slap of a finished film on the edge of the table, which you may remember from school if you're also of a certain age. The projector, however, is stored across town at the Chester County Historical Society Museum in the 1914 Chester Jail. Also in the booth, I smelled a horrid stink of pipe tobacco. Now I smoke CHEAP cigarettes, but this smelled like moldy clothes, cat pee, and old cheese. I also saw a haze in the booth. My late father-in-law, Alex Wylie, worked at the Powell as a kid and said that the long-time projectionist smoked a pipe like a chimney all day and night and that his tobacco smelled awful. When I described the stink cloud I had passed through, Pop (what I called him) said, yup, that was it exactly. The final experience was a bit funny and ties into the other experience I had at the Theater. On an informal "ghost hunt," in which every rule of professionalism was busted like whomp biscuits, a fellow actor led a group of about a dozen of us all over the building. As we all crowded into the booth, which was a bit tight to say the least, he said, "Let's shed some light on the subject!" and pushed the on button (it was a two-button switch). Now, there hadn't been a bulb in the recessed fixture directly overhead in at least twenty years. But there was a nest of pigeons containing roughly every "sky rat" in the tri-state area, if not the whole Southeast. When the click echoed in the normally quiet and empty booth, it startled every pigeon inside and they all decided to leave immediately. A dozen grown men and women ran screaming in full voice down the narrow and steep stairs and through the fireproof doors at roughly the speed of light. We all dashed across the street into the parking lot and watched what was actually about a half dozen pigeons fly off into the night. A Chester city cop drove by, looked at us, shook his head, and drove on. Don't fret about the birds returning home. One of the panes of frosted glass in the projection booth window was and is missing.

Well, that was enough excitement to send almost everyone home in a hurry. But someone had to lock the place up to prevent squatters and/or trespassers and I got volun-told. One guy went and checked all the door downstairs while me and the genius behind the light switch decided to make sure everything was ok upstairs and had me tag along, for luck I guess. While we're making sure any candles were out and such, he suggested that I go make sure to check that the doorway to the alley was locked. I shrugged and said sure. Now, the staircase to the door was simple. Four concrete steps with metal grips on the edge to a roughly five-foot by five-foot landing and then four more steps to the door on your left side. No biggie, right? Bull to the shit. I bopped my (then-skinny) ass down the first four steps like it was nothing. And walked into a choke slam. SOMETHING had picked up all two-hundred pounds of me about four inches off the ground by my neck. Now, I'm still just walking away. I could feel myself being choked and you could see the red marks on my neck where I was being held. After what seemed like an hour, but was probably thirty seconds, I got slapped across the face by somebody I couldn't see but they put every ounce of themselves into it. I mean, they reached back to Jesus and slapped me and they meant it. After the crack of skin on skin, and the visible handprint on my homely mug, the guy reached out, grabbed my belt, and yanked me back, laughing like he was in the throes of an ether binge. Rubbing my cheek and neck, I spun around and read him all the Riot Act in triplicate. Did you know you can use the F-Bomb as EVERY part of a sentence, including the punctuation? Well, I did that night, at volumes that likely scared Voyager One. Idiot boy finally stopped cackling like a hen laying a prize-winner long enough to gasp, "I just wanted to see if she was still here." The volume of my response made aliens flinch and drowned out a Spinal Tap concert, "WHO?!?!?!" He just said, "The cleaning lady. She HATES white guys." I gave him both love fingers and stomped out. But yes, the unfortunate lady mentioned above is apparently who took an immediate and vicious dislike to my existence that night. Luckily, I haven't seen her since.

Foster's Tavern

Foster's Tavern is a National Historic Site located just outside Spartanburg, South Carolina. In the antebellum period, it served as a major stop for travelers from Charleston and Columbia to Spartanburg and points north via the Old State Road. John C. Calhoun was a frequent guest during his service in Washington as were dozens of lesser political lights of the period.

The haunting at Foster's Tavern has only been reported in local media since the 1980s, but has been around since the turn of the century. The oddest aspect is the sound of horses' hooves on the roof. Now, no horses have ever been SEEN on said roof but why let that slow down a good tale. I expect this is the distant echo of some long forgotten drunken prank. The playing of a piano by invisible hands, as well as the inability of the piano to remain in place after being moved to a new location also trouble residents. Voices and footsteps have also been heard at night.

Since the tavern is now a private residence, I could not gain access to prove or disprove any occurrences, but I will share one odd event I witnessed. I was born and raised in Spartanburg County and grew up hearing legends of the haunting at the tavern. After college I lived in a former mill community named Glendale, which is near Foster's Tavern. Since I drove SC Highway 295 quite often between my parents' home in Lyman and my apartment in Glendale, I passed the site a couple of times a month. One night, as I sat at the red light at the intersection of SC 295 and SC Highway 56, I glanced toward the large brick building on my right and wondered if anyone still lived there. Almost in answer to my question, a woman's pale face appeared in the glass panel of the door I was looking at. Thankfully, the light changed and I took advantage of my place at the front of the pack. The house was occupied at that time, but the fact that I could see the wall and cabinets behind her THROUGH her gave a small bit of credence to the stories I had heard. I would urge you to remember that though Foster's Tavern is on the National Register; it is a private residence. Please respect the owners' privacy.

A Lost Tale

This story first appeared in the book *An Improbable Truth*, now sadly out of print but it was published by Mocha Memoirs Press in 2015. Both collections are non-canonical stories of the adventures of Sherlock Holmes and Doctor Watson, dealing with the paranormal and other high weirdness. If you've been at a Bar-Con panel in the last decade or so, you've heard the shuck story.... Which is more of an argument between my missus and I that dates from her role as editor of both anthologies. She claimed that I didn't need to use the word shuck to describe the ghost dog in the following because no one would know what the hell I was talking about. I loudly and vehemently disagreed, simply saying that folks could work in it out from the context. In case she's right (as she usually is), I'll give you a quick definition after the tale is told. I don't usually tell this tale when I'm spinning yarns because it's dense with odd names and sites from all over Devon in the UK. I think it's faithful to how Holmes and Watson would react in these circumstances in canon.

As ever, the tale is told by Dr Watson.

Enjoy…

The Case of the Haunted Branch Line

Following Holmes' exertions in France late in 1886, I had returned to my practice while he recovered his strength and mental acuity. Mrs. Hudson promised to keep me posted on Holmes' recovery and to monitor his resorts to the syringe. With the coming of the promise of Spring, Mrs. Watson resolved to take a tour of the Lake District with the wives of some other doctors of our acquaintance. Thus, when the press began to report on the strange events plaguing the construction of the Powerstock line of the Bath and Bournemouth Railway, I was well-prepared for the summons that came via a particularly ragged member of the self-styled "Irregulars" that Holmes wanted me at once.

I returned to the familiar grounds of Baker Street via hansom with a carpetbag in my lap, prepared for at least a week in Dorset. Not the least of my preparation included my faithful "Bulldog" with a full box of ammunition. As I paid the driver, I noticed that my shoulder had not pained me at all since the papers had flooded the market with increasingly lurid tales of ghosts and specters plaguing not only the railway track surveyors but the work crews themselves. With a nod to Mrs. Hudson and a request for some tea, I mounted the staircase to our apartment; realizing with a shock that I recognized not only the voice of Holmes, but that of his visitor as well. And it was not Lestrade for once! My pace quickened just in time to be greeted by Holmes with an exuberance he was not usually known for unless the syringe had been used too often.

"Dear Watson! Now we can begin to make headway on this puzzle as well as firmer plans! Watson, I expect you recall our guest, Brereton Roeblunel, from your days in the Maiwand. He is now-"

For once I could interrupt Holmes. "Yes, I do recall Mr. Roeblunel very well. After all, his survey of the proposed Maiwand Railway route is most of the reason I was there to get the wound that makes my shoulder aches in every fog in this fair city. I am also aware he is now the Chief Consulting Engineer for the Somerset to Dorset Railway and directly responsible for the route for the projected branch line to

Bridport. Sounds like he has kicked the hornet's nest, to use the Americanism."

The man before me was a good decade my senior and had had quite a career, despite my surliness. He had been the driving force in trying to build a railway line from Lashkar Gah to Kandahar over the Maiwand Pass. His refusal to treat with the Ghazis, nay even to speak with their chiefs with any respect they felt due, who controlled the area helped trigger the Afghan War. His further refusal to accompany the troops sent to assist his navvies served to make him less popular with the men than Ayub Khan - which considering Khan was commanding the native levies is impressive. Upon the Vice Regal Council deciding not to pursue the line, he returned to England at the direct request of the Duke of Earnscombe to serve as the engineer for the Somerset and Dorset railway line.

Holmes resumed as if I had not spoken. "Yes, of course, Watson, but Mr. Roeblunel is now a client with a most intriguing problem. Please explain, Mr. Roeblunel."

With that I gave Holmes' back a glare as he retrieved his slipper full of black shag to refill his pipe, but I took my familiar chair by the hearth and relit the pipe that had gone out since I left the cab. Holmes soon took his place on the divan, leaving the client to perch on a bullet-pocked-kitchen chair near the door to our rooms. After a moment of fumbling in coat pockets, Mr. Roeblunel found his matches and cigar, and after lighting it, began to speak.

"Dr. Watson, my apologies for your shoulder. I was young and foolish in the Maiwand. I assure you, I have since matured, if not aged a century since coming to Powerstock. Damn Dorset! Now, as Mr. Holmes may have mentioned, I am at present engaged in attempting to bring some glimmer of modernity to darker Dorset via the construction of a standard gauge rail line to connect Bath and Bournemouth and replace that abomination of broad gauge. Thankfully the Earl of Earnscombe is a modern man and has no truck with superstition. If only his fellows were so bright..."

"Very well, my good sir, but what of the case?" Holmes interjected sharply.

"Er, um, of course. As you have read in the better papers, construction of the line began from the Earl's estate south of Bath and the poor cottagers had sold all the actual rights of way at very reasonable rates, except for the area around Powerstock, one of the proposed Union Stations and link with the Midland. There, some young firebrand, bathed in the glow of Georgism, rallied the local yeomen against us with cries for fair value and land taxes. Damned young fool! I do declare, he is the root of all my troubles."

"As for ghosts, they are a mere memory of some undigested mutton, some overcooked pie perchance. At any rate, workmen soon began to report the most fantastic tales. Of trains on the old tracks, moving over tracks whose removal I personally ordered and witnessed. Phantoms seen in houses and fields, even ones too wet to support a mere babe in a basket. Noises like one of Booth's bands going through a foundry. Utter damnable balderdash. Mr. Holmes! Dr. Watson! You must prove all of this is merest tomfoolery, better suited to that village of fools, Gotha than the fine farmers of Dorset!"

Holmes leapt up and spoke, "Of course we will be happy to see what game is afoot for you! But with fair warning, we will report the truth, regardless of its inconvenience to you or any other. Now, the good doctor and I have final arrangements to make and some research to complete. We will be in Powerstock by dinner tomorrow. You and the Earl can expect our report in about a week or so at the most. Now, do give Dr. Watson the names of the young orator and any of your workers we will need to speak to on our arrival. Thank you and farewell."

With that, Holmes picked up his bow and violin and began to play an unfamiliar melody in a minor key, while I saw our guest down to the street to await the coming of his hack. His upset at the curtness of his dismissal and my lingering frostiness combined to make the conversation clipped and very quick.

The orator we needed to interview was one Paine Cobbett, reputedly the grandson of the reformer and reporter of the days of Wellington, and Roeblunel's most trusted man on the ground, Barlow Bouch, who trained under Stephenson ~~in~~ at the dawn of rail. After jotting the names into my notebook, I turned to mount the stairs to return to Holmes when Roeblunel spoke.

"Watson, do tell Mr. Holmes that these wild stories have no credence. Merest party tricks and magic lantern slides at best. That damnable Cobbett is the root of our worries and the key. Do mention to Holmes that the thanks of the earl and myself will be very remunerative in the case he resolves both puzzles satisfactorily."

With my blood up at the thought of this barely concealed attempt to bribe Holmes onto the wrong track, I threw open the door to find—him at his reading desk, surrounded by his commonplace books of clippings and tossing loose pages about like a booksellers in a typhoon.

"Holmes -" I began, only to be cut off in mid-breath.

"Watson, have you seen my copy of Bradshaw's? I have

doubts that Roeblunel's motives are such that I desire to be in his debt for anything, even a second-class fare. The man is at best a fool and at worst a bigger scoundrel than even you believe. Come, Watson, Bradshaw's, man!"

I turned and saw the volume lying half-buried on his chemical apparatus, holding a retort half-full of some noxious liquid labeled "E.P. from FWHM 1886-02" under the spout of some other device of Holmes' own artifice. I walked over and handed the volume over and resolved to tell him of the bribe.

"So, Watson, should I call Lestrade and tell him about us being bribed to frame a man who is likely to be innocent of any folly but youth? But of course not, Roeblunel has been infected with the modern belief that money will solve all difficulties, even those of a more metaphysical sort. I expect our difficulties have far older roots and more modern causes. Why, using inland towns as smuggling depots is not new! No one likes paying the excise and if there are profits to be made, man will find them. And I expect we may well find more to this than either of us expect once we have our boots on the ground. Now, what do you recall of these tales of ghosts and spectres?"

"Well, you have me at a sizeable disadvantage, even larger than usual, Holmes, for you have both memory and research arrayed against me and my leaky memory, but I shall attempt to answer. I seem to recall sightings of a ghost train, both before and after the Great Western's tracks were removed last year. Reports of an large number of derailments and accidents on a fairly flat and straight stretch of tracks over the years, at least one stone bridge collapsing. And various phantoms seen on and along the tracks. However, I don't recall any news about major smuggling rings being smashed by the excise men or the like however..."

"Excellent work, Watson, but you do recall the reports of a shuck in the area? A large black hound, serving as a harbinger of death on all who lay eyes upon it on some ill-omened farm path in the dark of night. Not to mention the salient fact that there were rumors of phantom funerals and reports of the Wild Hunt as well. All psychical phenomena well designed to keep the unwary or unwanted away from any place where mischief may be taking place. As you may have heard, I have assisted Mr. Myers with the Society for Psychical Research with some case investigation to keep my mind sharp after my exertions in Paris, including the capture of M. de Lernac following his attempted blackmail of some minor French military men. At any rate, I can tell I am boring you, so what of our arrangements?"

Holmes was wrong for once: I was far from bored. His

role in De Lernac's capture was completely unreported here, unlike that of de Lernac's escape from custody that led to the resignation of the Minister of Justice and nearly toppled the Republic. And Holmes dabbling in the supernatural! What was next? The sudden arrival of a Mrs. Holmes? At any rate, I knew Holmes well enough to keep my own counsel and simply said, "According to Bradshaw, we can catch a train direct from London at Waterloo Station to Bridport after supper and if we telegraph ahead before departure, we can have a trap and pair waiting to take us on to Powerstock on our arrival at eleven, if you do not object to dining on the train."

"No but I must ask why we cannot leave from Paddington? After all, the Great Eastern has its terminus there and it is the most direct route to Dorset and Dartmoor!"

"Yes, it is, but we must go direct to Bridport, unless you wish to spend the night at Bath waiting for a Special. Unless you wish to accept Mr. Roeblunel's offer?"

"A pox on Roeblunel! As always, Watson, your good sense and good humour saves the day! I saw when you arrived you brought your trusty carpetbag. Am I to assume you brought your pet as well?"

"Yes, Holmes, the Bulldog is in there with plenty of

ammunition. Though given the game we look to be pursuing, perhaps some holy water and silver bullets might do us more good!"

With that, we concluded our packing - well, Holmes did so; since I had already come prepared, complete with my old medical bag of Maiwand days. We caught a cab for Waterloo Station, where, as always, I paid for the tickets and sent ahead for both trap and room at Bridport and Powerstock by wire. Holmes sent two wires after mine but did not share the contents or the recipients of either with me.

As ever, the train disembarked at exactly 8 p.m. and dinner was announced just as we passed Chertsey Station at nine. It was served in the dining carriage and consisted of grilled beef steaks of a kind unknown to any butcher, undercooked for my taste but edible, green beans that may have been fresh if they were picked during the Crimean War, a cream of carrot soup that was alternatively scalding or tepid by each sip and palmiers that were largely cinders from the roadbed. The stout was serviceable and since the train was not full, the service was at least good and attentive. Holmes ate every bite and smoked two pipes to my one before jumping up and stomping towards the rear of the train, leaving me to my own amusement. I read the *Times* (yesterday's edition) and attempted to use the lessons of my acquaintance with Holmes on my fellow travelers. I must have found my companions less than engrossing, as he returned after an hour away to find me asleep with a lap full of stout, left there when the train took a bend a bit faster than regulations permitted, and a cold pipe between my teeth. However, my catnap did not bother Holmes in the least, as a small article at the bottom right corner of my long-forgotten paper caught his eye.

"By the Eternal, Watson, even when caught napping you serve more of a purpose than nine-tenths of your fellows! Look here - notice of a by-election for Poorton in Dorset. The Tory candidate is our old friend Roeblunel and his Liberal opponent is none other than Paine Cobbett! Most excellent scouting, my good man! We have managed to eliminate one likely suspect without even arriving at Powerstock."

"Now, let me enlighten you as to the news I have uncovered from the trainmen and crew. The true locus of the disturbances seems to be Eggardon Hill and the Brid Valley below. The actual line the crews are presently working on is a branch from Bridport to Weymouth via Dorchester, which is rather more of an undertaking than the shareholders or the Earl himself believe, hence the publicity that the line is only going from Yeovil to Bridport. Our path is clear...

AH! We must be approaching the station. Quickly, Watson, let us see to our bags. Our ride to Powerstock proper will not tarry long, given the outré circumstances."

With that we settled our account with the waiter (two shillings six pence) the two of us was reasonable, or would have been, had the food been as good as the beer) and we returned to our seats to gather our bags, which thankfully seemed to be undisturbed, at first glance. As soon as the train had slowed to walking speed, Holmes and I made ready to de-train onto the waiting, if deserted, platform as soon as the conductor announced Bridport Station.

Holmes led the way to the street-side where we made the acquaintance of Gale Whetham and his trap and pair. Holmes passed the man a pound note and asked him to take us to Eggardon Hill and to wait for us on the stone bridge over the Brid until he saw three quick flashes from Holmes' electric lantern, when meant we were on our way back to him directly. If he saw two quick flashes, he was to return to the station and wire Lestrade direct at the Yard with an immediate plea for all aid, without ascertaining our status first. Whetham grunted and took a long swig from his jug and swished his whip. The horses took off into the cloudless night, guided more by the full moon and habit than anything Whetham did. Whetham was best described as a character.

He wore a cloth cap, a frayed and patched corduroy jacket that might have been coffee-colored once and matching trousers, now the same color as the dirt coating his hands and neck. He was slender but sinewy, like farmhands all over the world. A hint of red hair peeked out from under his cap, matching the beard that was largely hidden by the foulest pipe smoke to ever waft into my face from close quarters. Not even Holmes' cheap shag could overcome it. I guessed this rough local had spent time in a workhouse or two in his day, as well as some time with the local constabulary under suspicion. But Holmes seemed to trust the man's wits, discretion and ability and I trusted Holmes like no man since my brother's passing, so I would trust Whetham as well. A loaded pistol can serve as a nice way to ensure a man does what is right, even against his inclinations. After about a two-hour ride over roads first improved by Caesar and left untouched since, we arrived at the bridge.

"Mr. Holmes, doctor. I will remain here until your signal, if the horses permit it. Those low clouds off to the south serve notice the Hunt may be out tonight sooner instead of later. If you two have the misfortune of meeting them, do hold the grass and keep your eyes averted, lest you be swept into their company. If I must abandon you, I will send your wire per our discussion earlier."

"Whetham, I could nothing else. I appreciate the advice, but I expect the mischief we encounter tonight will be far more corporeal than legendary. Do what you must, but remember our agreement. We must be carried on to the Three Horseshoes in Powerstock by morning for you to get the other pound you were promised."

"Aye, and I expect to earn them, but not at the cost of my mortal soul, Mr. Holmes. Godspeed and good luck."

With that, Holmes and I walked the few hundred yards to the foot of the hill, where the right of way was marked by a profusion of rags I had not seen anywhere but the Clootie Well outside my old boyhood home of Munlochy. It ended at the riverbank, but the footpath continued into the trees beyond. About one hundred yards behind us, the clearance for the right of way stopped, its location marked by a pile of creosote-soaked timbers of local lumber and a profusion of iron rails stacked head high. Holmes looked around and suddenly pointed to the far bank. Six men had just appeared from nowhere, carrying what looked to be by their efforts, a heavily-laden casket on the path before us. As the first pair of men stepped into the calm waters of the Brid, the mournful and unmistakable howl of a large dog broke through the silence behind us. Holmes spun on his heels and in one smooth motion, grabbed a stone from his feet and tossed it right at the hound, which appeared to be standing amidst the ties. That, or the stack of iron had suddenly opened two large red eyes and had gained the power of speech. As always, Holmes' aim was perfect and he struck the beast directly betwixt the eyes, only to be met by the ring of stone on iron. If hound there was, it was now gone. With an inward shiver, I recalled that according to lore, the first to sight a Shuck was to be the next to die. I decided to ask Holmes what he thought of such moonshine as soon as we were safely ensconced with some tea and biscuits before a fireside in Powerstock. After the rock twanged off the ties, I glanced over my shoulder and saw that the pallbearers had gone as quickly as they had come. With something of a start, I realized that I should have heard the splashing of their treads through the still water, but I had heard nothing but the hound's baying.

"Holmes, what the Deuce!" I whispered, only to be interrupted in mid-thought.

"Watson, by all means be quiet and see if you can approach the old rail bed of the Great Western line. I expect the rest of tonight to be much like the last few minutes and unless I'm very much in error the 2.10 to Bridport is en route."

"But, Holmes, those tracks are -"

"Yes, Watson, all the more reason not to tarry. Now, away and have your pistol as handy as your light."

With that, he headed up river towards the old wooden bridge. I sighed and turned to my left to flank the hill's base, with a quick glance up to its crest, complete with Stone Age hillfort, already old when Claudius Caesar sent his armies to cow the barbarians who lived in its shadow. As I picked my way through the brush to the gravelly remains of the fifteen-foot clearance for the abandoned broad-gauge line, I suddenly realized that the pallbearers Holmes and I had seen approaching the Brid were all headless. With a shiver, I clambered up the bank to the centre of the track and tried to orient myself. I decided to face away from the river, expecting whatever was to come would be coming towards Bridport to my rear. I noted with some inward alarm that the storm clouds we had noticed when we left Whetham's company were growing still larger and closer, though the moon still illumined the scene as well as any gas fixture ever filled a room. I reached into my jacket pocket to reassure myself that, despite traversing some rough country, my pistol was still loaded when I spotted a figure about a quarter mile from me walking my way. I distinctly heard the crunch of gravel under his hobnailed boots and saw the flicker of his red lantern even from that distance. At his nearer approach As he came nearer, I relaxed and walked towards him.

"Holmes, finally! Can we go back to Whetham and find a fireside and perhaps a whisky even? Some dirt floor cottage in Powerstock will be as welcome as Baker Street by this point. By the Eternal, too much of this uncanny furore is not good for one's mental state."

Much to my dismay, the approaching figure was not Holmes, nor could I ever hope to identify the poor soul. He was headless! But he was still able to approach and wave that lantern in an arc from hip to hip without spilling a drop of oil. As he drew to within some fifty feet, he stopped and turned away from me - not that I was ever a concern of his in this world - and began to frantically swing that infernal light. The distinct rumble and snort of an approaching train suddenly filled the atmosphere around me and led me to leap for the grassy safety to my left. Only when I landed on my bad shoulder did I recall that the tracks had been removed some ten years before and the last train scheduled on that line had crashed up at the self-same wooden trestle Holmes had gone to investigate. I also recalled never seeing an approaching headlight.

After checking again that my pistol and other parts were in working order, I slowly stood up, grasping the branch of a small larch that had crept to the edge of the gravel and looked around for my fellow wanderer, but saw no sign of him nor his lantern anywhere. Nor was the quiet of the night broken by the passing rattle of railway carriages or the click of heavily-laden iron on iron. After I had fully recovered my wits, I decided to report what had occurred to Holmes in the hope that he could make some sense of it all and I headed up the gravel towards the old trestle at a slow jog, trying to land on the crossties in order to avoid any further jostling. When I finally rounded the bend up to the trestle, the sight that greeted me was simply too bizarre for words, but I must attempt to do it justice.

Holmes was standing in the center of the old trestle some one hundred feet above the still waters of the River Brid, with his arms outstretched like some medieval saint in ecstasy, facing me but not seeing me. On the far bank, I witnessed the after-effects of a horrible smash-up. The engine hung from the trestle, four foot drivers turning in the empty air at a furious pace while the tender laid on its side on the trestle itself, steam billowing out in all directions like fog over Whitechapel from the Thames. On the tracks behind, two or three carriages had telescoped into each other like a set of Russian nesting dolls of the Czar's family. Women and children wept and looked into faces of the dead seeking familiar ones. Men ran all about, seeking to succor their fellows and offer any help they could. As I stood, awe-struck by the devastation before me, I decided to shout to

Holmes so we could offer our assistance. Just before the words left my mouth, I took another step onto the trestle itself and the horrors before us simply vanished like the passing of a magic-lantern slide in some third-rate music hall. As I stood there, mouth agape, Holmes suddenly appeared in front of me.

'Come Watson, let us signal Whetham and return to the comforts of Baker Street at once. There is no point is in going to Powerstock at all in this case. A simple written report should suffice to rectify matters for the Earl. Poor Roeblunel may not find it to be a pleasurable read, but such is life."

With that, Holmes made his way to the top of the hill and flashed his lantern to Whetham, while I remained at the foot, mouth still agape after the wonders I had just witnessed. Neither of us spoke during the hike back to the track where Whetham waited for our return. Nor did we speak to each other on the ride back, though Holmes chatted amiably enough with our driver, asking if he would rouse the stationmaster and wire the earl to authorize a Special to return us to London posthaste. Whetham readily agreed, though I think the promise of another Pound was the true motor of his quick agreement.

On our return to Bridport, we waited in silence while

Whetham completed his errand for Holmes. The stationmaster blanched until Whetham took him out of our hearing, and with a sideways look, explained where we had just spent three rather eventful hours. Holmes offered the man a few more coins for his trouble and the wire was sent. After some delay, surely caused by the fact that it was, after all, close to four in the morning, a response came in that our Special would be on site in the next hour. I approached Holmes to ask just what the Devil had just happened when he waved me away with a vague promise to discuss it all fully after we returned to Baker Street. I napped as well as I could, given the circumstances, but my time in His Majesty's Service had stood me well. I could still sleep anywhere, if a modicum of quiet was to be had. After the allotted hour passed, Holmes woke me with a hand on the shoulder and we boarded the Earl's carriage. Not even the prospect of a well-cooked breakfast could stave off the sleep I so craved, though Holmes told me later that the coffee was most excellent but the buns were a tad underdone, though plentiful. I awoke in time to have a quick cup of coffee before we pulled into Waterloo Station.

"Watson, I expect the earl and Roeblunel will meet us at Baker Street, despite my express wishes that I report in writing. I must ask you to entertain them while I attend to my toilet and get my thoughts well-arrayed to overcome their provincial objections Make no mention of what we saw at Eggardon Hill tonight beyond it being damnably curious business. And do ask Mrs. Hudson to prepare tea and cakes for our guests. I expect at this early hour; bad news may go down easier with a full stomach."

"Of course, Holmes. How long will you need? And I expect we will not be able to discuss all this between ourselves until they are gone?"

"Sadly, I expect we may not discuss any of it afterwards, unless you insist of course. But we shall see."

As Holmes predicted, Roeblunel and the earl were sitting in our rooms when we arrived. Neither man wanted to wait for Holmes to make himself presentable for guests, though my torn trousers nor well-scuffed shoes got not a second glance. Their shortness with Mrs. Hudson got the colour into both my and Holmes' faces and I almost escorted them to the curb but a glance from Holmes calmed me enough to request that Mrs. Hudson feed both us and our guests. As I was telling her this and calming her nerves, the Earl erupted like Krakatoa in the South Seas.

"Now see here Mr. Holmes! You wire me in the wee small hours of the morning with a demand that you report to me only in writing! No man has ever spoken to me in that manner and not lived to regret it! Now, damn it all, you will come in here and tell me what happened at Powerstock! I have a railway to finish and no time for dilettante detectives!"

"My good sir, you WILL make time for myself and Dr. Watson. YOU have directly disregarded my wishes in coming here and have upset my landlady with your expostulations. I desired to report in writing in order to spare you some of the sting of what I had to report, especially for Mr. Roeblunel. But since you have entered the den of the rattlesnake, you may as well feed on the venom. First, Mr. Roblunel's weak attempt at casting aspersions onto Mr. Cobbett was laughable on its face from the start. The discovery by my partner, Dr. Watson that they were to be opponents in a by-election sealed that completely. By the way, I do recommend you find another candidate to stand for the Tories in that race. Mr. Roeblunel is less popular than cholera in that district and will likely be swamped like a dinghy in a tempest by popular feeling alone."

"A damnable –"

'One more outburst from you, Roeblunel, and I will have Dr. Watson physically eject you from these rooms from that bay window opposite without benefit of clergy. Your engineering skills may have once been excellent but the years you have spent trying to redeem your failings in Afghanistan have been largely wasted. Until you met the Earl and decided that his greed would be your best hope of returning to the pinnacle of your profession. The attempt to build a line from Weymouth to Bridport would only assist the smugglers in avoiding the excise men while lining the pockets of those who built it. The financing was impossible to raise by private means on the Exchange, hence your need for the Earl. A small branch line from Bridport to Powerstock or even Poorton would benefit the smallholders and farmers of the region and might get you bought out by one of the larger lines, like the Midland even. But it would not sooth the bruise to your ego that the Maiwand left. I expect you had plans to extend the line all the way to Portland via a bridge if the money kept pouring in.

"Now, my good Earl, I recommend to you that you build a Chapel of Rest upon Eggardon Hill to lie the poor souls wandering the area to rest. I also recommend you follow the line of the Great Eastern for your line, though I would suggest you demolish the old trestle and find a fresh approach. Gale Whetham is a local man of some learning who has some very useful thoughts on the subject, having grown up there. Hiring mercenaries went out of style in this kingdom about the time we lost the American colonies. You could profit from George III's example. As to why I recommend this, suffice to say, the area is unsuitable for your purposes and only tragedy will result from any attempt to do otherwise. Now, gentlemen, I will post my bill to you and will expect payment within the fortnight. Goodbye."

With that, Holmes picked up his violin and bow and began to play scales. I escorted our still sputtering guests to the door, making a point to allow Mrs. Hudson to enter with the tray before they left and not offering them a single morsel. I returned and poured myself a cup of tea and snatched the largest cake and smiled. All would soon be back to what passed for normal at Baker Street. However, the howl of that hound echoed in my dreams for years. Not until the events that climaxed at Reichenbach Falls did it occur to me that Holmes had heard it before I had.

Now, as to what the actual hell a shuck is in British folklore.

A shuck is a black dog, usually about the size of a calf, mostly seen on sandy beaches, which it paces without leaving tracks, or just inland. To encounter a shuck is usually a sign of an imminent death, either of the witness or of a loved one. When the hound is heard to howl, the closer it is to the witness, the fainter the sound to living ears. Some reports claim the shuck only has one eye in the center of its head or it may breathe fire. I expect a goodly chunk of these stories are just tales told by smugglers to keep prying eyes home, but given that reports date back to the 1100s in some incidents, I'm inclined to believe that shucks are not just truly ghosts of one flavor or another, but are most assuredly good dogs.

A Tale

This story was written for this book. I've always been fascinated by the story of Tom Skelton aka Tom Fool, one of the last court jesters in England who served the Pennington family at Muncaster Castle in Cumbria. By all accounts, he was a real piece of shit and no one greatly mourned his passing beyond his employers. Given his casual cruelty, I thought he would be a good antagonist for the bisexual and gay couple in this story. I'm a middle-aged straight white southerner, but I have tons of LGBT+ friends who've had a crappy decade or so and decided that I'd try my hand at writing a tale where they weren't totally villains or victims. I think I pulled it off. Hope y'all like it.

Trigger Warning: There is some mention of sexual assault in this story.

Furness House, 1620:

John Will was a court jester more notorious than his

reputed master, the Fourteenth Viscount Crayton of Furness. John loved his pipe, any lady, high or low, who got within grabbing range, and a good joke at another's expense. If that joke meant some poor idiot got hurt, John found it even funnier. If they died, John would writhe on the ground guffawing like an escapee from Bedlam for hours. Yes, John Will was the ultimate jokester. And a homicidal maniac even for his bloodthirsty times.

When he wasn't cutting capers and making harshly personal jabs at his masters and their high-born guests for the outlandish sum of one hundred pounds per annum and free room and board, John sat on a three-legged stool under a majestic oak that was young when the Conqueror landed at Hastings on the road that ran to Furness town. It crowned the ridge on which the old abbey sat and was just high enough that even a man on horseback could not see the fork in the road below. One fork ran to town along the riverbank. The other led into a marshy bottomland with an unpleasant surprise. Just before the road to the left reached the river, the road had been overtaken by a swath of quicksand that was a good ten feet square and damned near as deep. A copse of trees and brush hid the fatal spot from passersby and a small set of rapids midway between the two made just enough noise to cover any cries for help.

Travelers and merchants who didn't pass that way on the daily had ample reason to be at the least neighborly, if not out and out overjoyed to speak to John. Because those who vexed him in the smallest manner, be it real or imagined, would be told about a shortcut to a ford that was no more than ankle deep. It would save them hours of trudging. All they had to do was take the left fork at the bottom of the hill. About once a week, John would borrow a gleaning hook and fish out whatever valuables he could. Of course, sending travelers down the wrong path to an early and sandy death wasn't the worst thing John Will did in life. No, the poor love-struck carpenter named Nick could testify to that.

Nick had the misfortune to fall head over heels in love and lust with the Viscount's youngest daughter, Damita. She was all of sixteen and he was pushing hard at thirty. The age gap wasn't the issue it would be today. However, him being of common birth and a laborer at that was. Damita was almost as smitten as Nick, but she did understand from watching her two older sisters get married to men their father chose that she had practically no say in the matter. However, she did know that John Will had her father's ear and if anyone could convince her father to let love conquer, he could. Failing that, John was devious enough to assist true love, if the money and other rewards were sufficient. However, Nick and Damita did not realize that there was a rival for Nick's affections, or at least attention. John Will himself. John Will had first spotted Nick when he arrived at Furness House two years before. Nick was about thirty years younger than John and John quickly realized that Nick was both naïve and ambitious. Those were traits John had spent decades exploiting in both men and women from the lowliest kitchen wench to at least one sitting Duke. As soon as John saw Nick and Damita exchange lovestruck stares and whispered vague promises, he struck, offering Nick his guidance and counsel. Nick quickly accepted,

Knowing that John had the Viscount's ear, Nick could not guess what his eagerness would lead to. John began by having Nick move into the windowless room adjoining his in the House, making sure that the door locked from the outside and that John kept the key on his person. After a few nights, John offered to train him in the ways of seduction so Nick could press his suit with Damita more vigorously. In this, John was merely following in the footsteps of men like royal favorites Piers Gaveston and the Duke of Buckingham or at the very least, hoping to make Nick like those fellows. Nick resisted at first and offered some violence, but John was far more cunning and cruel and swiftly wore him down, treating the younger man much like a wife. After about a month of this treatment, and moving no closer to the arms of his actual beloved Damita, Nick began to plot on his own and kept his own counsel. He still saw Damita on the sly and even managed to puts both hands and lips on her a few times before they were interrupted. At the end of the second month, Nick tired of his rough treatment at the hands of John. He had made no further headway with Damita, much to his frustration, and he had decided that John was more interested in his own pleasure than genuinely helping Nick with his suit. Soon Nick hit on a plan. One midnight, while John was visiting the privy after a bit more wide-ranging night of sport, Nick noticed a small sack under the foot of John's bed. He reached in and pulled out a handful of sovereigns. Math not being Nick's strong suit, he decided that he was now rich enough to take Damita over to Gretna Green and then set up house in another shire, away from the Viscount's discontent. The next day, while Nick was working on repairing a privy, John noticed a handful of his illicit gains from the quicksand was missing. Of course, his thoughts immediately turned to Nick and he decided that it was time to shift his focus and affections elsewhere. He also knew that he needed the Viscount's tacit backing, just in case, and knew how to get it. The opportunity soon presented itself.

Viscount Crayton was harried like a hawk is by sparrows. He knew he had to find a suitable match for Damita as soon as he could. He had both observed and been told about the lingering touches and glances between her and that low-born loafer, Nick. He also knew that young love needed to be quickly redirected back into proper channels, lest it flood the senses and lead to grave errors in judgement. Men could have mistresses, but women could not avail themselves of such an option, at least not until a proper heir had arrived. With these thoughts gnawing on him, John Will arrived to entertain the Viscount prior to dinner with their nearest neighbor, Shane, Baron Kerr. The Baron was a stout forty-five-year-old man who had outlived three wives and fathered ten children. Only two girls and one son had lived to adulthood and the youngest was the same age as Damita. Neither man saw an issue with the Baron marrying a sixteen-year-old, as both men needed legitimate heirs.

During his performance, John Will made sure to mention "saving the craft in the NICK of time," as well as other references he knew the Viscount would understand. When he mentioned what you had left if you cut the NICK off a Nicholas…a las(s), the Viscount stood and applauded his loyal gesture and nodded. He also slipped John fifty Pounds. He fully understood John's point and heartily approved. Damita would not be the first bride to weep at her wedding, be they tears of joy or sorrow. Over the next week or so, John made a studied effort to avoid Nick, but kept a sharp eye out to track his movements. He also sent two pilgrims returning from Canterbury to the quicksand for not laughing at a vulgar joke he made about the Virgin Mary. So he was in high spirits when Nick strolled up the hill to the backless wooden chair where he always sat Nick and Damita had figured out that the huge feast the Viscount was planning for Lady Day had nothing to do with the coming of a new year but was to announce her betrothal to the Baron. The young lovers had decided to flee to Gretna Green that night. Better poor and together than her rich and miserable.

John was of course overflowing with goodwill and advice. He quickly extracted their grand plan. She was to await John's arrival on horseback at her window and then she would spring onto the horse and off they'd go. The gatekeeper had been well paid (with my money, mused John) to keep the gate open and not to raise any alarm. They both thought the plan was foolproof, not foolhardy. John knew Nick owned no horse, so he offered to convince a stable boy to leave the barn door ajar and the stall holding Damita's mare unlocked to assist their escape to blessed matrimony. The whole time, the jester fed the fancies of the besotted youngsters. John had decided how to regain his lost money and put his erstwhile master into his eternal debt.

The stable boy was cowed into cooperation with a beating of epic proportions. No bones were broken and his face was untouched. However, the two plowmen John had bribed certainly left no room for discussion about what the boy's directions were. The barn was to be left unlocked but only the top of the stall door was to be left open and unlocked. The stable boy was given a shilling and told to head for the pub as soon as the dinner bell rang. He was assured of worse to come if any word got out or the directions weren't followed. The stable boy followed his instructions and left for the pub as instructed.

John slipped into the barn and let himself into the stall. He held the pruning fork over his head like a Saracen executioner and waited in the dark smelly stall. The mare stood quietly, munching hay. The leather hinges on the barn door squeaked like a mouse being pursued by a feral tom cat. No light crept in, but John knew it was Nick.

Nick made an error in judgement. He made no real effort to be stealthy, knowing the stable boy was gone to drink his troubles away. He reached the mare's stall in a dozen steps. He was a bit puzzled to see the door was not cracked like he expected but it did not dampen his resolve. Being with Damita as man and wife was his sole focus. When he found the lower stall door locked, he decided to try to reach in and pull the pin from the lock. When his gangly arm proved too short to reach it, he decided to climb over it. This would prove to be a fatal error.

Nick decided not to try to step onto and over the door, but to scale it like a farm boy going over a rail fence, by going over headfirst, bent at the waist and then throwing his legs over one after the other. The last things Nick saw in this life were the faint orange glow from John's pipe and its reflection on the blade just before it struck. His head fell onto the hay at John's feet while Nick's body was still lying limply on the stall door. John threw the head into the empty feed bag he had grabbed after he entered the barn and reached into Nick's pocket and retrieved the money Nick had taken from him. With a leer, John dropped one sovereign into the pooling blood at the base of the door. He then strolled back to the house, without a concern in the world.

John quickly went to the Viscount and after awakening him, informed him that the deed was done, leaving Damita free to marry the Baron. The Viscount groggily accepted the news and arose to give John his reward, fifty Pounds. John apologized for waking him but felt that doing so was wiser than giving him the news during the coming hue and cry. The Viscount grunted something about dark deeds being told in darkest night and immediately resumed snoring.

The next morning was a busy one at Furness. Damita arose, frantic after a sleepless night of anticipation that turned to dread as dawn drew closer. Two milkmaids entered the barn just after dawn to milk their charges and soon emerged screaming in shock and horror. The party of men they assembled hastily entered the barn and found the grisly remains. The stable boy was soon found in a still drunken state, with blood on his clothes. He had brushed against the fatal stall door while weaving way back to his straw mattress, but that would be enough to convict him, especially after John reported the theft of some money to the Viscount, including a few sovereigns. On questioning, the landlord of the pub freely mentioned that the stable boy had spent several shillings the previous night and bragged of doing John Will quite a turn. This seeming theft sealed his fate. The terrified lad was hanged over the road from a stout branch of John's oak, not far from his stool.

The Viscount sent a boy to the Baron to accept his proposal of marriage on Damita's behalf. Damita cried, cursed, and begged but her father stood firm. In less than a fortnight, the unhappy bride was nearly dragged down the aisle. Damita gave birth to two children, a boy and a girl. The boy lived to adulthood. She insisted at the top of her lungs that he be named Nicholas. Damita died giving birth to stillborn twins after four years of marriage, aged twenty-one. Baron Kerr died twenty years later following a week of tremendous debauchery in London for the opening of his town estate at age seventy. He was survived by Nicholas and his fifth wife.

John Will lived on for another twenty years and served as jester to the Viscount until his death from rabies. A fox John had caught and was trying to tame using torture turned on him. He was buried in the garden of the closed-up house under an impressive monument. In one of his last moments of clarity, he grabbed the Viscount by his beard and told him that Hell was much like Furness, as the gentry sat nearest to the fire. Then he more calmly and plainly stated to the Viscount that he would haunt the halls until the trumpet sounded if he was buried in a stodgy old churchyard.

Nicholas Kerr, the First Duke of Furness, inherited Furness House when his grandfather passed away. He never lived there, preferring the more cosmopolitan life in London. The only mark he made was to plow up the old garden and to have John Will's tombstone thrown into the quicksand. The house soon fell into ruin, used mainly by travelers in need of lodging in bad weather. During the rebellion of the Duke of Monmouth – when he tried to overthrow his uncle, James II in 1685 - loyalist troops accidently set fire to the main hall when a cooking pot spewed grease all over the hearth. As the troops fled, several swore they heard the cackling laughter of an old man and a few brave souls said they saw an old man in out of fashion striped clothes dancing among the flames and making rude gestures. No remains were found afterwards.

The Kerr family prospered in the decades after the fire. The third Duke made a fortune in the India spice trade and the fourth Duke invested wisely in a shipyard and a few railroads. Just before the lamps all over Europe began to go out in 1914, the Kerr family returned to Furness, rebuilt as a hunting lodge by the third Duke. The heir to the fourth Duke, Michael, Baron Eskshire and his family made it a home. Then Michael was sent to France. He managed to survive the war by virtue of being named a headquarters aide to Commander-in-Chief of the British Expeditionary Force on the Western Front, Earl Haig, despite being gassed by the Germans a month before the Armistice.

Sadly, when influenza reached Eskshire, the first victims were the Baron's wife and son. So, after recovering from being gassed and a fairly mild bout of the often-fatal flu, Michael returned to Furness an embittered near-invalid.

Furness House, 1920:

Michael Kerr was NOT in a mood for this today. Dr. Welsh, his physician, had come yet again to encourage his patient to do the therapy to improve his lung function. "Can't have a future Duke coming down with TB!" was the constant refrain that rang in Michael's ears. Meanwhile,

Michael knew his time was running short. He'd coughed up three lungfuls of blood since the good doctor's last visit. But to humor the old fool, the Baron did as directed... thirty minutes of jumping jacks, pushups, chin-ups, and such as the doctor regaled him with ghastly tales from the trenches followed by the latest London gossip.

Neither bit of palaver held the slightest scintilla of interest for the nobleman. He simply wanted to do the exercises, then return to his chair at the fireside and to his full snifter. Today, however, the doctor had an additional task in mind. A stroll around the grounds! God, thought the Baron, how long will this last? An hour? Two? After a lengthy coughing fit, soaking his navy silk handkerchief in blood; which the doctor blamed on the harshness of the Baron's choice of pipe tobacco, the Baron moved towards the door. Sigh, of course: the doctor insisted on tagging along. Apparently, the tale about seeing a German infantryman trussed up like a Christmas goose wrapped in all the barbed wire in France was not quite complete. The Baron shuddered, as if fighting off a passing chill, but actually with disgust. Never was he happier to have avoided the trenches than when the doctor started on one of these discourses about the bloody Boche. The Baron set off towards the gate, heading towards the old garden and site of the original barn, now long since turned into a mock folly. He told the doctor that they might walk to the old oak, if the weather held. This cut short the goriest of details and led the doctor on to a discourse on how all a gentleman needed in the rain was a good hat and a good navy grade wool overcoat. The only thing rubber was good for was car tires, if that. By the time the gate was reached, the Baron still had his wind and turned towards the oak. By happy accident, the doctor was waylaid by a neighbor's maid, weeping and begging him to come check on her mistress right after the turn onto the now graveled road was done. The doctor begged his leave and the Baron airily waved him off.

As the tree grew close, he thought spied an old man in antique blue and white striped livery sitting on a stool under the oak. In the time it took for the Baron to wave a farewell to the doctor and turn back, the figure was gone. Michael shook his head and walked on, intending to turn back once the doctor's Ford was out of sight. But he continued to the tree. He leaned on the rough bark, hacking and gasping from the overexertion. The autumn chill seeped into his bones, reminding him that he was no longer a strapping lad but a man nearing forty. As he gazed out over the valley of the River Esk, namesake to his title, he noted the old fork in the road, visible through the dead sedge, barely a hiking track now. A rude chuckle made him whip his head around, searching for the person who snuck up and ruined his wool-gathering. But the glade was empty and only the breeze spoke through the falling leaves. With a shake of his head, the Baron returned homeward.

As he approached the house on the cobbled drive, a loose stone caused him to misstep, almost making him fall face-first. Strong arms grabbed him about the waist and allowed him to steady himself. As he stood upright and turned to thank his benefactor, he was suddenly enraptured like he had been only once before... when he first saw his late lamented wife, Alexa. All blue eyes and bosoms, yet tall and as slender as a reed. He was face to face with an Adonis. No, a Heracles. Shaggy red hair, ruddy face, blue eyes, as broad as the barn he must have come from, but not fat. The Baron's mind went back in time, to school, where everything was topsy-turvy. New boys began on the bottom but rose to the top as time passed. Last year men left behind broken hearts as they discovered long forbidden fruit of a more conventional sort. But until then, the gleanings of those cold winter nights in communal rooms were instructional enough for most in the interim. Even once he had bowed fully to upper-class norms (no Bosie, he), he had returned to older familiar comforts that cold winter on the Somme. He had hoped that returning to home and hearth would drive those lapses away, but the figure before him swept away those thoughts as thoroughly as coming home to three funerals in a week. Michael was smitten.

Nick was intrigued. He'd walked from the old barn to the gate for centuries. As his spirit walked, it sought both the familiar landmarks and any trace of his beloved Damita. No one had ever noticed him even early on when he raised a hue and cry that should have awakened every living creature within a dozen miles and even did so physically. The man was handsome, if a bit scrawny for his taste. Nick knew he was deathly ill, which may have allowed them to share physical contact. An odd feeling buzzed in the back of Nick's mind. The man was too damned familiar to be unknown to him. Somewhere on the other side of existence, Nick felt stirrings he had not had in three centuries. Michael managed to regain his composure and thanked the young lad for the assistance. He asked who he was, aiming to reward him for the good deed. The man simply said "Nick," as if that answered every question. After another stammered thanks, Michael turned towards the house. When he glanced over his shoulder, the drive was empty. He entered the house, mind racing.

Nick smiled as he walked to the old barn. A glance towards the old oak showed him that John Will was sitting on his stool fuming. He lacked the will to appear and misdirect the mortal. This futile display of rage made Nick's heart glow with uncut joy. He knew what his job was now, and he saw his time as an untethered spirit coming to an end. Soon enough, he'd join Damita in paradise and watch John Will roast on a spit in Hell or spin adrift on an eternal storm trying to out-howl a thousand demons in the gale. Either one suited him just fine. But first, he had to wait for the proper time. The gentleman had to be ready in all senses for what was next.

The next afternoon, the good Dr. Welsh returned for another round of therapy and more horror stories. Michael had had a very bad night. When he slept, he had vivid dreams of interludes with his strange benefactor, vivid enough that the nocturnal emissions would have been hard to explain to his late wife. After each one, he woke with a hellish coughing fit. They lasted for what seemed like hours. He had ruined three silk handkerchiefs and after the last, he snatched up his late wife's pillow and likely destroyed it and the case after soaking it thoroughly with bright red blood. The bed looked like an autopsy at a cheap brothel. When the doctor tried to cajole him into another stroll, Michael feigned a faint. The doctor decided not to press him, fearing the loss of a steady source of payment too soon. Instead, Michael asked after his neighbor. The doctor informed him that it was merely false labor caused by overexertion and that both mother and babe were fine.

Rather than hear about who was cheating on who among the smart set in London or about the glories of battlefield surgeries, Michael asked the doctor what he knew about Furness House. The doctor told him about John Will sending travelers to the quicksand, about the burning of the house and the supposed figure in the flames. He made a passing mention of the frustrated lovers but knew no details, even when gently pressed. Michael asked plainly if the doctor had heard of any legends of ghosts at Furness. The doctor pooh-poohed ghosts as hogwash and hokum meant to separate widows from their wages or worse. After that definitive statement, the butler called Michael to his dinner, expressing dismay that the doctor was still there, as the staff had only cooked for the Baron. The doctor took the hint, stating that he would see Michael in two days, since tomorrow was Sunday.

After dinner, a rare steak and a baked potato and a small salad and three slices of pound cake washed down with a bottle of claret, Michael got a sudden impulse to take a stroll towards the site of the old barn. The butler cleared the dishes and nodded, his concern well hidden. He had seen the Baron staring longingly into nothingness for several minutes the previous afternoon. He had heard from the young chambermaid during their pillow talk after luncheon that very day about the mess found in the Baron's bed. The butler had seen the Baron's older brother lose his senses to syphilis a decade before and feared that another Kerr was doomed to the same fate of madness, if TB didn't kill Michael first. How the doctor couldn't see the signs that the Baron's lungs were literally tearing themselves apart... The butler shook his head and sighed. Perhaps he could have a word with the doctor on his arrival Monday after luncheon. Gwen would have to be satisfied by their after-breakfast tryst. He'd make it up to her.

In the gathering dusk, Michael made his way slowly towards the gate, hoping to avoid the near fatal stone. As he passed the barely visible cellar hole of the old barn, Michael felt a figure fall in step beside him. Without even a glance, he knew that Nick, the carpenter (how the Devil did he know that?) had joined him. He blushed like a schoolgirl and asked how Nick had fared since their last meeting. Nick said he'd stayed busy but offered no details. For some reason, on the way back, Michael asked Nick in to have a drink and chat. The Baron had some ideas on improvements, especially to the old road and that huge old oak. Nick readily agreed and let Michael lead the way.

Michael caught the butler lighting lamps in the study and asked him to bring the decanter of Scotch, some ice and water, and two glasses. The butler, seeing only the Baron, asked if he was certain the Baron needed two. Michael told him sharply to do as he was told, or some staff might be sent to the London house, bleak and empty before the season. The butler quickly did so and thanked Michael. He lit the lamps in his master's chamber and returned to ask if his services would be needed for the remainder of the day. Hearing a firm no, he quickly retreated to Gwen's chamber to tell her of the latest bad sign and to enjoy her company.

Michael offered Nick a seat on the leather sofa, mentioning it was covered in elephant leather. Nick exclaimed, "Where did you even find an oliphant to skin?" Michael chuckled quietly. His young friend was if not unearthly, then at least unworldly. Michael regaled Nick with family lore as far back as he could remember through the mists twenty-year-old Scotch tossed up. Nick seemed to listen intently, questioning Michael about the names of wives especially. Michael began to tell the tale of Damita's wedding to Baron Shane when Nick grew even paler in the flickering lamp light. As the grandfather clock in the hallway began to strike twelve, Nick rose with a start and bolted for the door. Michael gave chase into the entryway, where the worst coughing fit he'd had struck. Nick paused at the door and said, "The doctor is mad and useless. I shall see you Monday afternoon and prove that to your satisfaction." With that, as Michael bent at the waist hoping to drag air back into his ragged lungs, Nick vanished through the locked door, unseen.

The next morning, the butler arose early to tidy up the study. He found the decanter drained and the ice bucket dry. One glass had a faint amber ring in the bottom and had left a white ring on the mahogany desk, The other still had three fingers of damned fine Scotch in it. Seeing it as part of his duty, the butler drained it at a gulp.

Despite the fit that nearly killed him at midnight, Michael slept the best he had since the spring of 1914. No nocturnal emissions, no bloody hacking coughs, not even a snore. He awoke with not even a hint of hangover, which given that he and his guest had drained a full decanter was impressive. The Baron went to church and even tipped the vicar ten shillings for his excellent homily on David and Jonathan.

Everyone who saw him was impressed by how good his color was and his vigor. Several old folks shook their gray heads and whispered that even dead cats bounce. But even they were pleased at the seeming improvement. On returning to Furness, Michael requested a platter of cold cuts, bread, and cheese be left for his use and then sent the staff off on a much-needed spree day. At church, he'd told the landlord of The Capering Kid to be sure to open up and to stay open.

He was to feed all comers and keep the ale coming. Of course, the Baron would pay the bill when presented as always. And yes, even the fine if the village busybodies sicced the constable on the festivities. Michael returned home to an empty house, grabbed a novel and his provisions and settled in for a quiet Sunday. As dusk approached, he walked to the front door and looked towards the gate. Nothing stirred, not even a breeze. No young man strutted up the drive. Michael sighed like an abandoned fling and returned to his book until he heard the staff returning full of watered down lager and eternal stew. The flirting and joshing continued down the hall to the servant's quarters, leaving the Baron alone.

That night was as peaceful as the previous one. The Baron ate like a true trencherman for breakfast and lunch as well. He even did the exercises he knew Dr. Welsh would press on him without prompting. He was in fine fettle. Just after high tea, the doctor arrived, full of hope that the Baron had finally made a positive change and would soon be on the mend. But the doctor knew that The Duke's suggestion might cause some upset.

Michael met the doctor at the door, glistening like a Greek athlete at the first Olympics, but of course not nude. Michael told him how good he had slept the last two nights, not mentioning the bloodbath from earlier that week or his guest. The Doctor mentioned that he had heard of the Baron's welcome return to church and how pleased everyone was with his appearance. However, the Doctor said he had gotten a wire from the Duke in London on Sunday. He wanted Michael to apply to the King for the post of Consul at Tangiers for his health. The Duke had decided that the Doctor was wrong about Michael's diagnosis and that the lad had damned TB, not any inflammation. Michael sat down heavily on the sofa and put his head in his hands. "I refuse. I've finally getting my legs back under me here after a rather dicey few years. If I do have TB, then I'll die as quickly in Tangiers as here!"

With that outburst, the front door flew open of its own accord and Nick entered. He crossed in front of Michael and placed a callused finger under his chin. All the doctor saw was a door fly open in calm weather and his patient look up with a damp face and a weak grin, that soon turned into a beaming smile. Nick squatted before the Baron and simply asked if he was ready to go away from all this. The Baron looked into his eyes with pure uncut longing and whispered, "Where is your home?" Nick said plainly, "The grave. None but the grave for these many centuries." Michael leaned forward, threw his arms around Nick's thick sun-leathered neck, and chastely kissed him on the lips.

The doctor saw the change in his patient's demeanor from impotent upset to shy joy. He saw Michael embrace empty air and then fall back on the sofa with a ghastly rattle from the stricken chest. After a few seconds, the doctor jumped into action, checking for a pulse, ripping his shirt open and massaging the fevered chest and calling for brandy and help. Michael and Nick watched all the frantic activity with looks of bemusement from the open door. They then turned and descended to the drive. There Damita and Alexa embraced their true loves and each other. Then the foursome strolled towards the gate, vanishing before they reached it.

Right after the gentlemen met the ladies, the ancient oak on the hill gave out a tremendous groan and fell across the lane. A screech of agony, like that of a songbird caught in a hurricane, rang out and was cut off as quickly as it arose. At the base of the stump, a three-legged stool toppled and rolled down the sedge covered bank, into the quicksand below.

Swamp Girl of the Congaree

The story of the vanishing hitchhiker has been around since the dawn of the automobile. Although it may vary slightly from place to place, the basics remain fairly constant. And yes, nine and nine tenths of the vanishing hitchhiker tales are utter bullshit, just like Crybaby Bridge. But a few have risen from urban legend to actual folklore... Larry Stevens, Resurrection Mary up in Chicago, Lydia up near Greensboro and a handful of others. The story generally begins with a young and attractive lady, usually wearing a dress that was stylish at least a generation ago, standing on the side of a quiet, once busy highway on a rainy or stormy night. A young man invariably stops and offers her a ride. The destination given by the young lady is always in one of the older residential neighborhoods in the nearest city of any size. The lady usually gets into the back seat and does not respond to repeated attempts at conversation. By the time the car arrives in the city's outskirts, the young man has to ask his passenger to repeat her destination. When he turns to ask, the back seat is empty, except for the jacket the man offered his passenger. The young man continues to his passenger's destination, only to discover that she had been killed in an accident that same night at the spot where she was picked up years before. Occasionally, the jacket leaves with the passenger and is retrieved from the young lady's headstone. This tale is probably America's most common ghost story. The only real competition it has is the ubiquitous "Crybaby Bridge." Many of these tales have a basis in fact but have grown into urban legends.

Due to its rural nature, South Carolina is home to more Crybaby Bridges than phantom hitch-hikers, but the state does have a few. The story of the Swamp Girl of the Congaree dates back prior to World War Two and is mentioned in the files of the Federal Writers Project from the 1930s.

Our story begins with a young Black nursing student driving from a late lab at South Carolina State University in Orangeburg to Columbia on U.S. Highway 601 in the late 1920s. Not having been around then, I cannot testify to the accuracy of the accounts, just the common elements. I believe the current Congaree River Bridge was built in the late 1940s. The night was stormy, cold and a bit foggy. As the young lady was crossing the Congaree River into Richland County, her car hit a slick spot and she lost control and likely hydroplaned. The car caromed off both sides of the bridge, eventually slamming into the abutment on the Richland County side of the river. (The bridge is located just north of the junction of the Wateree and Congaree Rivers, above Lake Marion.) The better-known Gervais Street Bridge over the Congaree is located near downtown Columbia. At some point, the young nurse-to-be was thrown from the car and into the river. A few days later, the car was recovered, but the body was not.

A few months later, a young couple was passing the same way in similar conditions when the wife spotted a figure on the roadside just after the bridge. Being a more innocent time, the couple stopped and offered assistance. The young lady requested a ride to an address on Pickens Street in downtown Columbia to see her ill mother. When asked how she came to be standing beside such a remote stretch of road, the young nurse, whose uniform was covered in mud mumbled something about car trouble. The young couple could not recall seeing any abandoned vehicles but simply assumed they had been focused on watching the road in such nasty weather. The wife tried to make small talk on the drive into downtown, but the passenger did not respond. As the car began encountering traffic, the husband glanced back to enquire about the best route to take when he nearly wrecked the car. The back seat was empty, save for a small muddy puddle behind his wife. The doors were still locked and the windows were up, but no passenger was present. The wife became very upset, as did the husband. However, a desire for answers led the couple to continue to Pickens Street to determine the tale behind their strange encounter. The mother, of course, had been dead for weeks and the family stated that the couple had not been the first to pick up the young nurse, who was still trying to see her mother.

Other odd events have been recorded in the area of Bluff Road (S.C. Highway 48). Notable among these are a horse-drawn carriage that races and plays chicken with cars, figures seen in the swamps and a bridge where cars are prone to stall out. Y'all… the area around Congaree National Park is freaking weird as Hell, Go in early spring or late fall, enjoy the hiking and camping and enjoy some peace and quiet… and maybe some general weirdness too.

My encounters with the Swamp Girl have been very similar to the one described above. My first encounter occurred on a stormy autumn night in the late 1980s. As I have mentioned before, I am a huge fan of so-called short cuts and back roads. While returning to Lyman from a weekend in Charleston, I encountered an accident on I-26 near Orangeburg. To avoid the traffic, I decided to take U.S. 601 to S.C. 48 to I-77 in order to get to Columbia and get back on I-26. At no point did I expect to have an encounter with anything out of the ordinary, as it was already late and I am not overly fond of deer on back roads in the rain. Shortly after crossing the Congaree River, but before I turned onto S.C. 48, I saw a rather attractive young lady in an old-fashioned nurse's outfit standing on the shoulder of the road. Thinking that the girl had been to a costume party and recalling that I had seen just one other car since leaving the interstate, I decided to give her a ride to the nearest pay phone as my good deed for the year.

I stopped about ten yards from her and she walked to the car. As I opened the back door to let her in, I saw that the starched white skirt was soaked and very muddy. She explained that she had had some car trouble and asked for a ride to Pickens Street in Columbia. She also asked if she could lie down and rest in the back since she had put in a long night at work. I said sure and off we went. After I crossed under I-77, I remembered that I did not have a map of Columbia with me and turned to wake her and get directions. Imagine my nineteen-year-old reaction to an empty backseat. Well, empty except for a puddle of smelly rainwater and thick mud across the fabric. After I stopped at the next gas station and calmed down, I remembered where I had picked her up. I decided not to add my name to the lengthy list of folks who had disturbed her family and continued on my way.

My second encounter was merely in passing. My wife Rachel and I were en route to see some friends in Charleston when we heard about a major accident at the junction of I-77 and I-26. Naturally, I decided to avoid traffic and headed down Bluff Road toward U.S. 601. Just after we got off the interstate, the long-threatening clouds burst. Shortly after we passed the entrance to what was then the Congaree Swamp National Monument, I mentioned my last trip down Bluff Road to my wife. Naturally, she blasted me for picking up a hitchhiker and doubted my honesty! After a few minutes of chat about such things and several good-natured (I hope) questions about my common sense, the topic died off as my attention returned to watching the wet, winding road and looking out for deer. Just after we turned onto U.S. 601, my wife gasped. I asked what was wrong and she said nothing. On reaching the interstate, I stopped to grab some much-needed caffeine and a potty break and decided to find out what had upset Rachel. She told me that she had seen a figure in a white dress walking down the grassy shoulder of the road. As we passed the figure, Rachel said she could see the trees behind the figure through the figure, hence the gasp. I was very much determined to go back when Rachel informed me that I would have to choose between a loving and happy wife and a long dead nurse. I made the right decision, as Rachel and I are still married.

The Bloody Bonnet at

Blue Hole

Hey kids! Do y'all remember when ghost stories used to be a huge part of Christmas celebrations? Like Andy Williams sang in *"It's the Most Wonderful Time of the Year"* in 1963, "There'll be scary ghost stories and tales of the glories of Christmases long, long ago," well, this humble tale is part of my contribution to bringing that tradition back. Not just because I like the idea, but because it gives me more chances to tell ghost lies for money. I mean, it worked ok for Charles Dickens, right?

This is one of the few Christmas ghost stories I tell year-round. It came about when Braxton Ballew and Sarah Black, better known as the world's best Victorian Goth chamber metal band, decided to record their album, *Winternight Whisperings*. Braxton asked if I could provide a story that he could improv on his electric double bass to over my narration. After a bit of hunting, I found this story. I think it works very well. Track down the record, because it may be the only way you can have the experience of Braton making me sound amazing without coming to hear it live.

Back before the Civil War in what they called the antebellum days, up near a little Georgia town called Varnell, there was a main road that ran, called the Federal Road that ran from Ringgold, Ga to Varnell and points beyond. And one Christmas Eve, some folks say around 1833 or so, a stagecoach driver was making a midnight run from Ringgold coming back to Varnell. It was late. It was stormy. He was cold and so were his passengers. He was working the six horses out front pretty good. About halfway to Varnell, the horses stopped in the middle of the road. No good reason. Couldn't tell a thing that was going on. He thought it was a bear. Looked up, horses would not move, nothing moving in the underbrush. He laid on the whip. Gave it to them for all they were worth. And, you know what happened? The horses would not move for love or money. Until finally, after he laid a couple open, they moved forward into a brand-new sinkhole that had just opened up in the road called the Blue Hole. About seventy-five foot wide and deep enough that when the stage went in; stage, driver, passengers, and horses, and all, none of them has been recovered to this day.

But, kind of a funny story, now the paved road, which I believe was called US 41, bypasses the Blue Hole but it's still there, all one hundred and seventy-five years later. But if you go up that way on a hike or out deer hunting or something, you may see a headless figure looking mournfully into the Blue Hole because supposedly the horses got so irate at the application of the whip that they kicked him. And one of them kicked his head clean off. And he comes back and marvels over his act of folly trying to get those horses to move.

Now I say the passengers and the coach, and the horses vanished without a trace, but that's not exactly true. Some folks say that a bloody bonnet and a broken horse whip were found on the bank of the Blue Hole. but if you go up that way now, reports are you'll hear the crack of a horse whip. You may well feel the rush of the carriage as it goes past, trying to keep that Christmas Eve appointment. But the most likely thing you'll see is that poor gentlemen staring into the Blue Hole wondering where his life went so terribly wrong.

Gates' Ride and

DeKalb's Stroll

The battle of Camden occurred on August 16th, 1780, when four thousand continentals and militia and two thousand British and tory troops collided just before dawn by accident. General Horatio Gates commanded the patriot forces and General Cornwallis commanded the British. Gates was the newly minted commander of the southern army after "he" (not Arnold or Morgan) won the battle of Saratoga in NY state the previous year. Cornwallis was three months removed from capturing Charleston and its whole garrison. The battle was fought about halfway between Camden and modern Kershaw (I know where that is!) Off US 521 and is largely unchanged. However, the road running by the site is Flat Rock Road, a two lane stretch of blacktop.

The battle was a disaster for the Americans. A quarter of Gates' army was killed on the field or captured and most of the militia may still be running for home. Among the dead were Baron DeKalb, who does have an actual ghost story.

Gates fled the field right after the British broke the American left wing, less than an hour into the fight. He arrived in Charlotte, about sixty miles away around midday. He was, as they say, picking them up and putting them down. About two days later, he reached Hillsborough NC... another hundred or so miles away from the scene of the defeat.

According to legend... ahem... If you are on Flat Rock Road between Macedonia Batist church and Flat Rock Baptist church, especially near or on the bridge over Grannies Quarter Creek, about an hour or so before dawn on the 16th of August, you may hear the frenzied and pounding hoofbeats of a laboring large horse racing towards you and fading as suddenly as they arrived. It's possible that a century or so ago, you could have actually seen General Gates on his mad dash to the safety of the hornets' nest, better known as Charlotte.

When I got the job as Branch Manager at the Kershaw branch of the Lancaster County Library in June 2024, it occurred to me that I wasn't far from the bridge in question, so I went down bright and early on the morning of the 16th, just to see, as it were, what might develop. I parked at a wide spot on the shoulder just past the bridge, which ain't nothing spectacular. I mean, it's just a concrete slab bridge with little concrete guardrails. As I stood in the middle of the road, already regretting coming outside in August in South Carolina as the sun peeked over the pines, I heard the steady rhythm of horse hooves coming hard, but I was the only living thing visible for at least a mile in any direction. Just as I turned to head back to my car, I felt a cold chill race through me, and I noticed that the hoof beats were damned near deafening. Just that quick, the chill and noise faded away. After an involuntary shiver, I walked back to my car, thankful for the AC and headed back to Kershaw for a biscuit and coffee.

Since I mentioned Baron DeKalb above, I'll give his ghost story as well. Baron DeKalb came to assist the Americans in their struggle against the British in 1777 with his protégé, the Marquis de La Fayette. He was made a major general in the Continental Army and given command of a regiment of troops from Maryland and Delaware after serving at Valley Forge. He was assigned to the Southern Department under General Gates and joined him on the march to confront Cornwallis at Camden. As a token of respect for DeKalb, Gates placed his experienced troops on his right wing. Sadly, this meant Gates had placed his inexperienced militia on his left to square off against Cornwallis' best troops. And the rout commenced. The entire American left bolted on the first charge, led by their commander. DeKalb tried and failed to rally the regulars, but fell with eleven wounds, mostly from bayonets. Cornwallis offered the services of his personal surgeon, to no avail. The British allowed their prisoners to bury DeKalb on the field.

Fast forward to 1825, General La Fayette has returned to visit a country enraptured by him and his heroic legacy. One of the hundreds of stops made by La Fayette on this tour was at Camden to dedicate a marker to his mentor at Bethesda Presbyterian Church in March. According to legend, the mortal remains of Baron DeKalb made the six-mile march to Camden the night before the ceremony, interning themselves under the marker just before dawn. Legend says you may see the Baron marching along US 521 or along Flat Rock Road. I've made that drive several times and haven't had the pleasure of seeing the Baron. When I do, I'll be sure to thank him for his service.

Court Inn - Gone but Not Forgotten

Camden proper is home to a fairly large number of ghost stories. One of my favorites is the story of the old Court Inn that was located on Mill St. at E. end of Laurens St. Sadly, the ravages of time laid waste to the site and it is now gone. This story is one of the older tales extant in South Carolina. The source I found it in was the Federal Writers' Project guide to South Carolina, *South Carolina: A Guide to the Palmetto State*, that was published in 1941. These state guides are an amazing resource for what life was like in pre-war America. One of these days, I'm going to finish my book compiling all these stories into one volume.

To Lausanne clings the legend of the 'Grey Lady,' ghost of Eloise DeSaussure, who pined away in a French convent, where her Roman Catholic father confined her because she loved a Huguenot. A gentle soul, she nevertheless pronounced a curse on her parent, who com-

mitted suicide when his wife died soon after his daughter. The 'Grey Lady' first appeared to Eloise's brothers in Europe the night before the Huguenot massacre in 1572. Disguised as a monk, one escaped to America. When tragedy forbodes, the 'Grey Lady' still appears at Lausanne.

The reason the story of the Grey Lady intrigues me so is simple. The two bronze lions that once guarded the drive to the Court Inn now grace the South Carolina State Library in Columbia. Given my choice of profession, I've spent decades going to sundry meetings there. The lions are named Sol and Edgar, named for Sol Blatt and Edgar Brown, two long time appropriators and powers in state government. Every time I go to the State Library, I want to ask them if they remember the Grey Lady, I also wonder if she walks Seante Street when bad things happen in Columbia or South Carolina.

Did Sherriff Meek Lay a Ghost?

I first came across this tale while I was working on *Ghosts of the South Carolina Upcountry* back in 2005. Yeah, I'm old, now hush. I could never narrow down where exactly Gordon's Old Field was, so I couldn't use it then. But me and the amazing goldendoodle George Bailey finally tracked it down thanks my love of old maps and roads. But first, a bit of background.

Adam Meek was born in 1760 and served under Colonel William Bratton during the Revolution. He rose to the rank of lieutenant and was universally respected. He served as the second sheriff of York County South Carolina from 1790 to 1793. Most people date Sheriff Meek's encounter with the ghost of Gordon's Old Field to this period. As far as whom the ghost was or why he had returned from the dead, no one ever knew…

The ghost in question had a rather fixed schedule. Every night just after dusk, the spirit passes along the road through the open field from one edge of the woods to the other. Upon reaching the edge of the woods, the ghost would vanish as soon as he appeared. Since the ghost did not appear to be in pain or panicked, no one could explain why he would appear there over and over. No record has been found of any violence on the site, before or since. Sheriff Meek had his curiosity aroused and decided to investigate the haunting. Only one of the witnesses he questioned admitted feeling any fear, not surprising considering that these men had just fought off one of the best armies in the world and had tamed what was a virgin wilderness less than fifty years before. Sheriff Meek waited in the field for the ghost to appear and walked beside it talking until the spirit vanished. Adam Meek never revealed what was said that night to anyone, even his brother James. Within a month of this meeting, Adam Meek left the area for a few weeks. Friends, family, and neighbors all assumed that the ghost had claimed the sheriff as its victim. After two months of wild speculation, Adam Meek reappeared, in good health but he never volunteered any reason or explanation for his disappearance. What is known is that the ghost of Gordon's Old Field never returned to disturb the tranquility of the Bullock's Creek area again.

As to where Adam Meek went and why, I have no more information than Rev. West or Dr. Moore. My personal belief is that, like many ghosts I have either encountered or read about, the spirit at Gordon's Old Field could not rest until whatever unfinished business he had on Earth was done. Old Southern tradition has it that if you ask a ghost what it wants in the name of the Lord (or the Holy Trinity or Jesus Himself), the ghost must tell you the truth and answer. Perhaps Sheriff Meek did this and informed the poor man's family and hometown of his death. Or he merely paid an overdue bill.

At any rate, having driven through the area on Walnut Street out of Hickory Grove towards the intersection with McGill Road a few times over the years, I can say that the area around the intersection always seems to make me want to speed up just a little, especially right at dark on foggy fall and winter evenings. Maybe something didn't get Adam Meek's message and is waiting for the right time to reappear? Now, the last time I went up that way something strange happened. I decided that me and George Bailey would go for a ride since Rachel was out running around with her sisters, likely going to a movie. For some weird reason, we wound up on McGill Road just before dark. Since George Bailey was just a puppy, he needed to poop after having been trapped in the car, which made him a bit anxious. So, I found a wide spot on the shoulder, hoping the car wouldn't sink to its axles after a week of hard rain, grabbed a poop bag and his leash. Well, George paced a bit, did his business, and then locked on... something in the field across the road. I didn't see a thing, but he was locked in like someone was walking by, watching their every step. I managed to get him back into the car, but he decided to go investigate, whatever the hell it was. So, he bolted, yanking the leash out of my hands. Thankfully, since we were in the back of beyond, there wasn't any incoming traffic. If there had been, I'd likely be worm food at the hands of my blushing bride. I caught up with him pretty quick. It was easy since he was just sitting about one hundred yards into the field staring at the tree line just beyond. I still saw nothing and snatched him and put him in the back seat of the car and we headed back to Chester. That reminds me, I need to take George Bailey on a ghost hunt or three. He may have better luck than I do.

High Strangeness at Manteo

Back in 2002, my wife Rachel decided we need to go to a concert… David Bowie supporting the album *Heathen*, a damned good record and well worth a listen even now. The only problem was that the nearest show was in Manassas, Virginia. In August. Outdoors. During one of the worst heat waves in the history of weather forecasting. Now, Manassas ain't exactly walking distance from Chester SC in optimal conditions. It's only six hours as the crow flies. In 2002, at a robust thirty years old, that was nothing, even with my back messed up. Then the variables started. Her friends Susan and Samantha had bought tickets too and they wanted to carpool with us. From Charleston, Johns Island to be more precise. Now, I don't mind a good ride but an extra four hours in the car was pushing it. Susan's mom said we could all pile into her station wagon, so yay for sparing my beat-up Mustang the wear and tear. BUT she said only Susan could drive. My back tried to argue but lost. Still, I could hang with that. And, oh, one more thing, their friend Zigs had also bought a ticket and wanted to make a road trip of it. I was like, the more the merrier, until they said she was working at the Lost Colony play in Manteo... in the Outer Banks. So, heck, what's a FOURTEEN-hour drive one way? So, we worked out that we would come to Johns Island, hook up with Susan and Samantha and stay overnight. Then we'd head up to Manteo and pick up Zigs after the show and crash for the night. We'd head to Manassas before first light, see the show and then reverse it. No big deal. Heck, I'm a grown man, I can handle it.

Things went fine until we loaded up to head to Manteo. Samantha insisted on having shotgun... the whole trip. I had hoped to be able to do shotgun a while to lay the seat back and stretch my legs and back, but at least I was trapped in the back seat with my darling. We got to Manteo and found our hotel at like 10 p.m. The show didn't get out until 11 or so. Ugh, but I knew that hanging around the hotel waiting for Zigs to call would be simply putting off our ability to get some sleep before the sprint run to Manassas. So, Samantha decided to crash and me, Rachel, and Susan headed over to the theater to wait on Zigs. Now, the theater is set in some woods and there is a line of rope lights leading back to the dorms for the cast and crew. Susan parked in the gravel lot as close as we could get to the end of the walk. As the show was finishing up, I saw a figure dart behind a tree about a hundred yards from the edge of the rope lights. He was older, bald, and had a white Van Dyke beard. He wore at the very least a black shirt. Just as I headed towards him, I heard Rachel gag. Now, I'm as psychic as a brick but Rachel seems to have a touch of the gift as it were. Sadly, for her, it manifests as nausea. Now, here is a minor but kinda important detail. As I mentioned it was high summer in the Carolinas, and we were basically in a coastal swamp in a helluva heat wave. Normally we'd all be eaten alive or carried off by mosquitoes or worse. Not a bug buzzed, bit, or even landed for the two hours or so we stood there. Another point to remember is that there wasn't a breath of a breeze. So, explain to me how my wife's short hair, dyed blue if memory serves, reinforced with something called hair cement, moved like it was caught in a gale? This was the last straw for the ladies, and they announced they were going to sit in the LOCKED car. In the AC. And I could come or not, but if anything, else weird happened, they were gone. I futilely gestured towards the now-vanished figure but my pleas to chase him fell on deaf and stubborn ears.

Now, the hauntings at Fort Raleigh (the site of the actual

183

Roanoke settlement) and at the theater complex have been recorded for over a century. People have reported seeing figures in the woods, hearing voices speaking both English and Native dialects, and being touched. In the backstage area, props are moved, figures in period garb have been seen in off-limit areas, and voices are heard coming from empty halls and rooms. In the dorms, personal items are moved, even into other people's rooms despite locked doors. Faucets are turned on by invisible hands, figures have appeared in hallways and even in bedrooms. I guess combining a theater, with all the paranormal activity that stirs up, with the site of a tragedy like the abandonment of the Lost Colony and the removal to CROATOAN might stir up some ghostly activity.

I'm not going to get into all the crazy theories about what happened to the Lost Colony. I personally think that once the supplies got low the colonists decided to stop waiting for the return of folks from England with more and went to stay with the Natives on Croatoan Island nearby. I mean, they did leave a note. Given that the Spanish had already established colonies and made expeditions into North America at this point and that the Spanish and English were at war, going to stay with a people who had actual warriors wasn't the worst idea ever.

However, the most famous bit of ghost lore from Manteo is the White Doe. Virginia Dare was the first English child born in America. Supposedly, she went to Croatoan with her mother during the evacuation and lived to young womanhood. While living there, she fell in love with one of the braves and he returned her feelings. However, a rejected suitor for her affections went to one of the tribal shamans and basically, if I can't have her, no one can; make it happen. So, after the lovers had announced their engagement, the shaman cast his spell. When her fiancé came to get her for the wedding, Virginia had vanished. The brave never married, longing for her return. After a few months, the chief ordered the braves to go on a deer hunt to refill the tribe's larders. Our broken-hearted brave was widely seen as the best hunter in the tribe and so he was made leader. After a few days of success, our lover had not yet killed his deer when suddenly, a white doe walked out of the trees into a clearing besides a small stream and drank. The hunter raised his bow and fired a fatal shot. As the doe fell, she turned back into Virginia. Her lover carried her body back to the village and then walked into the ocean as penance.

Back to our road trip from Hell, I couldn't chase mu new friend through the woods, and I didn't see the white doe. But Zigs finally down the trail with I believe all her worldly goods in hand. I mean, blankets, a small cooler, a backpack, a purse, the kitchen sink, Jimmy Hoffa… it was a bit much. But we got her and her stuff into the car and went back to crash for a few hours. For the run up to Manassas, I still couldn't get shotgun privileges, despite my back giving me thirty-one flavors of Hell. In fact, I had to ride the hump (of the automatic transmission) in the back seat from Manteo to Manassas. Rachel and everyone else but Susan slept the whole drive up. Oh, and everything Zigs brought… she had to have handy, so we couldn't stash it in the back. Despite all the driving, my aching back, and not having fun with my ghost friend, the show was balls-out awesome. Blue Man Group, Busta Rhymes, Moby, and of course, the man of the hour, the Thin White Duke blew the faces off the entire sell-out crowd. Despite the fourteen hour marathon, the misery of having to ride in the back seat for all of it, getting maybe four hours of sleep over two nights, paying horrible prices for water during the hottest day on record in Northern Virginia, and sitting in the sun for six hours, it was the best concert I've ever been to. Now, I was tired for at least a week after, but it was a damned fine road trip all in all. I mean all of us still speak to each other, except for Samantha. She kinda drifted off to do her own thing. Such is life sometimes.

Part Three:

Family Tradition

TO PAPA –

IN MOURNING

Still sticky Southern summer night
Lightning bugs and mosquitoes
Buzz through the twigs of the dogwoods
and leaves of the privet
The lights from the mill
Glow like a second sunset hours past.

Meanwhile in a house on the Mill Hill
Black vinyl recliner
On screened-in porch.
Tousle-headed and cowlicked teen
Lies on a wooden porch swing,
Bare feet dangle twanging the chains

Cigarette ashes on rust colored carpet and pages of
forgotten book.

While Papa sits like some newly enlightened Buddha

"Chaw" stains on his flannel shirt and chair alike.

Breath comes like dry leaves

Tossed in a halting breeze in the storm.

Love palpable like a living thing

Mind sharp but body shutting down,

Being devoured by itself

Organ by organ.

All the tales told,

Nothing left unsaid

While silence stays, still pristine

The teen rose and with a hand clasp

And kisses on the forehead,

Left for the real world

Already as bone-weary and jaded as his mentor.

Two from Grandpa...

Finally

My grandpa (my mom's dad), Carl Wilson, was a very cool dude and I hate y'all didn't get to know him. He gave me my first nickname... Tallywhacker. I had no idea why folks thought it was so funny as I got into school, until some forgotten grown-up gently explained it to me. But that was his sense of humor. I mean, he was a World War Two vet (served in the Navy and more on that in a bit), graduate of my alma mater, Wofford College, a chemist and more. I mean, he was a performing professional water skier while me and my grandma were working at the Florida School for the Deaf in the Fifties. Expert ballroom dancer, helluva guitar player, master gardener, crack shot, martial artist and more. Now, he wasn't perfect, and he didn't tell many tales until I was an adult, but he could spin a yarn almost as good as I can. He was always proud of me, from school achievements to my books, my storytelling (which he thought was funny and he was always shocked that I got paid for it), and my choice of wife. Heck, he liked Rachel better than he did me I think... but most everybody does. Anyway, after the death of my grandmother and the continued loss of his vision to macular degeneration, he lived with my parents for a while before he moved to assisted living.

A few years back, I got asked to tell tales at the Middle Tyger branch of the Spartanburg County Library up in Lyman and mom and dad roped grandpa into coming along. They promised him food after, of course. Now, the Middle Tyger branch was MY library as a kid: I read literally every book they had when they were in the small wooden branch in town in Lyman. Yes, even the Harlequin romances. Hell, I learned to ride a ten-speed carrying sacks of books in traffic from my hours and hours spent there. Anyway, the fateful day arrived, and I had a decent crowd and mom, dad, and grandpa were all in the front row. On the way to the car afterwards, he told me I had done a pretty good job and that he had two "spookers" for me at supper.

The first one he told me dated back to his service in the Navy. He served on a landing craft in the Philippines right after McArthur returned. They basically were in charge of clearing out the Japanese troops who had taken to the hills to avoid surrendering after the Allies retook the islands. He said it was scary as hell trying to convince a fanatic with a rifle to surrender if you were armed with a four-foot rattan stick and a Colt 45 pistol, even if there were ten of you and one of him. One night, he was manning the engine during a routine patrol in some harbor when a voice came down the tube from the bridge, The voice had a very distinct Boston Yankee accent. He was ordered to set the engine on Full Stop. Being eighteen and a fireman's mate… he did as he was told. Grandpa said about a minute after the boat stopped, a rather pissed off voice with a mountain accent even thicker than his (as he pointed at me with a grin) roared, "What the blanking hell are you doing? Why the blank did we stop?" Before grandpa could shout back, another voice said calmly, "Sir, looks like an anti-submarine mine has come unmoored from its chain. If Wilson hadn't stopped us…" The other voice came back and more calmly ordered full speed astern. It was only after grandpa was off duty and in his hammock that he realized that the first voice he'd heard was that of the Captain he'd had when he first joined the ship. Who had been dead three months after a sniper got him after a failed attempt to get the Japanese soldier to surrender. If that voice hadn't been heard over the engine noise, y'all wouldn't be reading this…

The second story actually freaked me out. He said that back in the early days of World War Two, he helped out at the Feed and Seed store in his hometown of Inman. One rainy day, his boss since his other helper, an older Black man went to the train depot over in Lyman to pick up a delivery in the boss's big Ford coupe. Now, according to Grandpa, his boss made and ran shine, so his car wasn't exactly built to factory specs. The guy set off down what is now State Highway 292. Apparently as he crossed the bridge over the North Tyger River, the car got away from him a bit and he went airborne. One thing led to another and the car came to rest in a creek in a gully, on top of the driver, who was killed instantly. Fast-forward a decade or two and my grandparents bought the land that backed up on that very creek and that contained the fatal spot. All went well until the late 1970s when Grandpa happened to engage his neighbor in idle chat over the chain link fence. Grandpa mentioned that the guy looked like ten miles of bad dirt road. "Carl," the neighbor said, "I ain't gonna be around much longer. I've seen the Black Man and you know what that means." Grandpa said no, no he didn't. According to the neighbor, if you happened to be fishing or doing work around that creek and saw an old Black man in bib overalls walking towards you who then vanished, you had three months to get your affairs together because you were doomed. Grandpa chuckled and told the neighbor that he'd probably live to be a hundred and two and not to worry about it. I vaguely remember the neighbor dying kinda sudden-like but I had never heard of the Black Man. As we sat at dinner that night, it dawned on me that I spent an awful lot of time in those woods as a kid, so I asked where the wreck happened. He asked if I remembered the log that went over the creek to where the parcel my great-granddaddy farmed behind them was. I said yeah. And then he said right about there. I smacked him on the arm and said in high dungeon, "Why didn't you ever tell me I was taking my life in my hands every time I took the shortcut and ran around back there?!?" He grinned and just said, "Hell, I didn't believe in that nonsense. The neighbor had a heart condition and three kinds of cancer. Besides, you're still here and so am I."

Grandpa is missed by all of us. I hope he and my grandma (Mema) are having a blast in Heaven and that they'll put a good word in for me.

From Mother with Love...
So Nice I Used It Twice

Much like Grandpa, my mom didn't tell me any spooky stories from my childhood until I was an adult. My theory is I was such a handful that she didn't want to make me any crazier than I already was. Regardless, this story has made such a belated impression on me that I've used it as inspiration for two separate stories in *Creek Walking*, my Southern Gothic short story anthology that Falstaff Books put out a while back.

I was still a babe in arms, so this story has to date to late 1973 or early 1974. Mom said we were living in a mill hill house in Jackson Mills, next to Welford, South Carolina. She was home with me and that Daddy worked third shift at the mill over in Lyman (this is before he started at Southern Railway). It was right at eleven thirty at night because the news on Channel Four had just gone off and Ed McMahon had just hollered, "Here's Johnny!" I apparently was sacked out in my crib next to the couch dreaming tremulous dreams because I never even flinched.

Right as Johnny Carson started his monologue, mom said she heard heavy footsteps on the wooden porch, like somebody wearing work boots, and then the screen door flew open like it had gotten unlatched in a storm. Right after that, she felt the window behind the couch rattle as someone kicked the front door open... but didn't mess up the door frame or lock. I find this hard to believe, but my mom swears that all this happened just like she told it.

Now, one thing my folks had done to the house was to put down some throw rugs down and a carpet runner down the hall This gives me a chance to explain the layout of this palatial estate. You had a set of concrete steps that led up to a wooden porch with posts at the corners and next to the steps. A two-by-four rail ran the length and width of the porch about waist high. Just inside the front door was the living room. Next to the door was a double frame window. A door through the living room next to the TV led to a small galley kitchen. The hall ran beside the kitchen and the bathroom backed up to the kitchen. Then two bedrooms at the rear of the house with the back door at the end between them. Mom and Dad slept in the room on the right side. "My" room was across the hall. Hell, fancy, right?

Well, back to the night in question, mom heard a scraping noise like metal on wood join in with the stomping footsteps down the hall. About ten or fifteen seconds later, though mom says it felt like an hour, the same thing happened to their bedroom door that had happened to the front one. She heard a loud gurgling moan and a bunch of thumps. By this point, my mom was cowering in the far corner of the couch clutching me to her chest. Now, if you've met my mom in real life, you know exactly how unlikely this actually is, but she swears it happened. After the last thump, the scraping and footsteps returned up the hall and the front door slammed shut as suddenly as it flew open. Then a heavy thump rattled the window again, like someone had just sat down on the edge of the porch at the steps. After another minute or two, me and mom apparently jumped in the car and got to my great-grandparents house over in Lyman in about a minute, mom said. Lights and TV left on and door wide open. Mom called dad at work and said that we were moving that morning and where she was. Dad tried to mention things like a lease and it being a Friday night and such and mom just said, "I'm staying here until we find a place less creepy. YOU can stay here or there." They moved out that morning and that was that.

When they turned the key in, mom asked about what had happened to cause all the fun a night or two earlier. The owner explained that back in the 1920s, an older man had gotten a job at the mill after his farm up in the mountains went belly-up. He and his much younger wife moved into the house right after it was finished. The man got a job at the mill as a spinner on second shift. Since his wife had been to school for a few years, she was hired as a secretary in the front office. Now, her boss was about her age, handsome, had a car, and wore cologne. He didn't smell like sour sweat, Mail Pouch tobacco, and bootleg whiskey. He also didn't cuss her about her cooking or not having a dozen babies yet. So, after some sweet talk and little gifts, and rides in his Oldsmobile convertible, an affair started. They would have trysts in a closet just off the office, on rides to the country on their lunch break, and as the affair got more heated, at her house after work. None of the coworkers or neighbors were going to say a word. The depression had begun and work was harder to find than decent liquor. Her young lover had the power of the purse and damned near life and death. So, most nights, that big Oldsmobile would pull up, the two would stagger up the steps in a clinch, and retreat to the marital bed. About ten o'clock, the man would leave for his house over near Greer and the older man would stagger home about eleven or eleven thirty.

On the fateful fall night, the older man left work as usual, but he was hotter than a bushel and a peck of peppers just out of the garden. A new hire, some youngin who had been fired and blackballed from mills in Gastonia, Honea Path, Lando, and Lancaster for being a Communist and a gossip had spent the whole shift telling the husband all about what his young thing of a wife was up to while he was risking life and limb. The husband resolved to just beat his ass tomorrow before shift. He expected the supervisor would understand that he did it to protect the company and he wouldn't get fired for the fight. As he came around the corner, he saw the Olds sitting there and hung his head. The smart-mouthed punk had been right as damned rain. Well, the husband thought, might as well settle all this hash once and for all. So he climbed the steps and grabbed the ax sitting on the porch rail that he used to cut firewood and to kill chickens for Sunday supper. Then he threw the screen door open while he kicked the door in. He stomped down the heartwood pine hall, dragging the ax in his right hand. The giggles, groans, and whispers continued to float up the hall despite the racket the man knew he was making. They did have the decency to pull the bedroom door to, but he kicked it in regardless. He found the boss man on top of his wife, both of 'em as naked as the day they were born, except for his argyle socks and her sensible flat Mary Janes. The husband swung the ax and buried it in the man's back, causing him to gurgle and moan as his dead weight fell on the bride below him. After another two or three blows, the scorned husband dragged the corpse onto the floor and stared at his thoroughly ruined wife as she screamed and wept for mercy. Then he struck her three times with the ax. He stomped back up the hall, slammed the door behind him and sat down heavily at the top of the steps and wept. He dropped the gory ax on the porch. He knew at least one neighbor had heard the ruckus and had called the sheriff on the party line. Hell, he already heard the sirens passing the mill.

When the cops arrived the man simply said, "Yeah, I did it. Sumbitch made a damned fool of me and ruined her beyond belief." He went to the county jail in Spartanburg, was put on trial without a lawyer. He confessed over and over. About six months later, they hanged him at the big prison in Columbia.

According to mom and dad, the house is still there, and it was for sale the last time they drove past. So if you looking at making a move to the Upcountry...

Papa Visits

My Papa, or great-grandfather, Talmadge Kimbrell, was my beau ideal of what a man was when I was a kid. I'm named after him, and I've tried to live up to his example my whole life. I like to think he'd be proud of how I turned out. He taught me how to drive a tractor, shoot a squirrel rifle, kill a chicken and gather eggs, and basically spoiled me bone-rotten. To this day, every time I see a Levi Garrett pouch of chewing tobacco I swear I see him. I missed him terribly even almost forty years after his passing. But I do think he's kept an eye on me all these years later...

In late November 1997, I was a nervous wreck. I was in graduate school finishing up my course work and starting on my (still-unwritten) thesis. Of course, being young and dumb I was also working seventy some hours a week at Radio Shack. And, oh yeah, I'm getting married to boot. Now, I knew the getting married part was a good idea, but I was a mite concerned. I mean, I could barely keep myself alive, and

I was going to willingly submit another person to the struggle, not to mention having to live with my crazy ass? And of course, like every other major event in my life to that point, it was a stress ball and a damned comedy of errors. My father-in-law, who liked me just fine until I proposed to his baby girl had made his disdain for the nuptials clear. Hell, I was half-convinced he would cold-cock me at the altar. Being poor, me and my groomsmen rented our tuxes because we were fancy and that was a hot mess. One groomsman's tux didn't have pants. My baby brother, who wore a forty waist back then, had pants with a twenty-four waist… and forty length. Two tuxes had no studs and my best man, the world-famous Bill Roddey, wouldn't even try his on until the day of the damned wedding… so as to not jinx things, he said. Oh, and I was trying and badly failing to quit smoking. To the point of wearing four or five high test nicotine patches at various strategic spots.

So, the night before the wedding, I'm lying in my bed around midnight in my crappy half a duplex apartment outside Chester, South Carolina. The neighborhood wasn't the greatest, so I had two deadbolts on the front door and my broom handle in the track of the sliding glass door. My apologies to the sliding door manufacturers of America, but the damned things come from the factory with busted locks. Think about it, when you rent a place or buy a house, they hand you your keys, your deed, and a cut off broom handle to put in the sliding door.

From my bed, I could see the hall between it and the bathroom, the bookcase between the kitchen and the living room, and the fridge. I have a big ole forty-four-ounce cup of sweet tea on my hip, a cut crystal ashtray on my chest with my cigarettes and lighter next to it, and I'm reading some enthralling tome like the *Alphabetical Biographical Directory of Left-Handed American Land Surveyors from 1700 to 1950*. I used to love to read stuff like that before bed, back when I could read two-point type and didn't need glasses to read street signs because even if you fell asleep reading it, it's not like you had to back track to find the plot, just re-read the page. Oh, and just a dab of nightmare fuel for y'all, especially if you've seen me in person, I sleep naked. Y'all are welcome.

As I lay there, trying to chill out enough to crash, I happened to glance up and my blood froze then boiled. SOMEONE was standing in my damned kitchen. I saw the side and back of an orange and white trucker hat, the arm of a black pair of glasses, a brown bomber style jacket, and gray slacks. Near as I could tell, it was an older white guy. I reached under the bed for the golf club I kept there just in case, remember I know I'm not damned crazy to have a gun in the house (I don't want the demi-colon tattoo for aesthetic purposes). When I did this, the following happened. The big gulp of tea spilled everywhere. The ashtray and cigarettes fell off my chest onto the carpet. The tome I was reading fell on the little toe on my left foot, breaking it. And I lost my dang place to boot.

I leapt from the bed with the club in hand (it was either a putter or a nine iron, I can't remember) and erupted into a steady stream of educational profanity, making helpful suggestions of what the guy could do in gory graphic detail at volumes likely audible in Europe. Just as I got my second wind, the figure turned towards me, and I blew all my fuses and vapor locked my feeble mind. The man was my great-grandfather. Looking like himself before prostate cancer worn him to a nub. He gave me a grin, tipped the bill of his Mascot Homes cap, and walked towards the front door. Well, this shit was just unacceptable as all hell. I remember hollering, "Hold on old man. We got all manner of stuff to discuss!" as I bolted to the living room.

When I reached the back of what had been his old recliner, I realized that the room was empty. In a daze, I walked over and checked the deadbolts… both were locked tight. I now realized my toe hurt, so I limped to the sliding glass door to check the broom stick, and it was still in the track. I confess I cried like a baby with colic and a dirty diaper for about two or three minutes and I whispered, "I miss you, Papa." But after I pulled myself together, standing in my hallway, sopping wet, my toe throbbing, I realized that I felt much better about this whole wedding deal. We were in love and it would all work out. The tuxes, her dad being cranky, all of that would just be stories to tell as things went on. And it seemed to have worked out for the best as of this writing, almost thirty years on, Rachel and I are still extremely happily married. In my expert opinion, Papa just knew I was under duress and wanted to check on me. He'd never been to Chester in his life, and I know he hadn't ever even seen that apartment, but he knew I needed him. I haven't seen him since, but I expect he still keeps an eye on me and puts a word in when I need it.

Sleep tight…

About the Author

Tally Johnson is an award-winning storyteller, folklorist, and author. He is the winner of the Caldwell Sims Award for Excellence in Southern Folklore from the USC-Union Upcountry Literary Festival. He currently resides in Chester, SC with his wife and fellow author Rachel and their fur baby Mr. George Bailey.

Other Works by

Tally Johnson

Arcadia Publishing

Ghosts of the South Carolina Upcountry, Ghosts of the South Carolina Midlands, and Ghosts of the Pee Dee.

Falstaff Books

Creek Walking

Prospective Press

Civil War Ghosts of South Carolina